Saving Sweet Sienna

By Amber Fawn

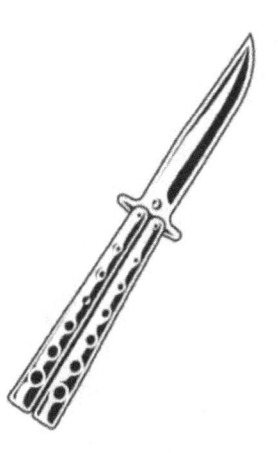

ISBN: 978-1-3999-8792-9

Readers note: 'Saving Sweet Sienna' is book 2 in the 'Orchid's children' series. This book is not a standalone. I highly suggest reading book 1 'Consequences' first, in order for the storyline to make sense.

To the man who calls me 'sweet'.

CHAPTER 1:
QUICK ESCAPE
Marcus

Fuck. That's about the only thought my mind can articulate right now. The red and blue lights relentlessly flash across the car park, stabbing at my eyes like shards of urgency. I take a quick breath, glancing around to assess the scene. The eerie puddle of blood spreading beneath Millie's head, a dark pool illuminated by the harsh lights. I watch as a police officer pulls Skylar from the mangled wreckage, her complexion drained to a deathly, pallid white.

As he shoves a now-handcuffed Skylar into the back of a police car and slams the door shut, her eyes meet mine. Her gaze, once fiery and defiant, now holds a cold, haunting depth. I smirk at her. I must admit it feels pretty good to not be the only one in the 'murderer-club' anymore.

The other police officers begin striding towards our group, their authoritative presence sending tension rippling through the air. Dean and I exchange a quick, concerned look as the sirens continue to wail through the car park; a tormenting reminder of the night's chaos. At that moment, my eyes are lured back to a narrow gap between the police cars. It's a risky proposition, the passage so small that doubt creeps in. But I have no other option. I briefly turn my head to instruct Sienna.

"Hold onto me really tight, sweet." With that, my sweet squeezes her little arms tighter around my waist and leans her head against my back. My motorbike rumbles beneath us as I rev the engine, its power ready to surge at my command.

With a resolute nod to Dean, I break away from the group, my eyes fixed on that narrow escape route. The concrete walls of the car park seem to close in as I approach the gap, the challenge ahead magnifying with every inch. The pulsating lights and sirens create a surreal soundtrack to my escape, the world around me warping into a high-stakes battleground. As I navigate through the perilously tight gap, the wind howls in my ears, and time itself seems to slow. The narrowing passage becomes a needle's eye, and every calculated manoeuvre is a dance with fate. Adrenaline courses through my veins, heightening my senses as the blurred scenery becomes a kaleidoscope.

I grit my teeth as we somehow successfully slice through the space, the narrow gap grazing the sides of my legs and bike mirrors. The world beyond the car park unfolds before us, the city's streets a familiar canvas. Behind, the coppers shout, the echoes of their voices mixed with the sirens as yet another chase begins.

They're almost getting boring at this point.

A grin creeps across my face as I surge ahead. My bike responding to my every command, weaving through the labyrinth of city streets. With every twist and turn, the "fuck" on my lips is both a curse and a celebration, a raw expression of defiance against the encroaching forces of capture. I'm fucking untouchable. This chase is not a pursuit; it's a celebration of my prowess, a reminder that I am the architect of my escape. That I'm simply too fucking good for them. They don't realise that this is the easy part for me. The thrill courses through my veins like a drug. I've already escaped.

Catch me if you can, dickheads.

As the sirens wane in the distance, a triumphant laughter escapes my lips. I'm leagues ahead. A vanishing phantom in the city's nocturnal embrace. Sienna loosens her grip slightly and leans away from my back. It's subtle, but I notice. It brings me a surge of arrogant satisfaction. It's like she's acknowledging that I've got everything under control, that she can relax because I'm here.

And damn, does it feel good.

"You okay, sweet?" I ask. Sienna huffs out a single sarcastic laugh.

"Never been better."

"Hey, we're alive, aren't we?" I counter.

"Well, Millie isn't." Her cold, honest response catches me off guard. I can hear a tinge of guilt in her voice. The scene was truly horrific, and Sienna shouldn't have been subjected to such a distressing sight.

"It was a terrible accident, there was nothing we could've done."

"That doesn't change the fact that she's dead because of us. We made her come, Marcus."

"She chose to be here, Sienna. Yes, we needed her help, but it was her decision to give it to us." I say, my voice firm but empathetic. "If she didn't show up it would've been Dean instead."

The truth of my words and the unsettling reality of life's demand for sacrifice, hangs between us. Sienna's eyes wander off to the side.

"I know," she admits, a resigned acknowledgement in her voice. "But it doesn't make it any easier, does it?"

"No, it doesn't," I concede, understanding the complexity of emotions that must be swirling around in her pretty little head.

As we approach the outside of the city, I reduce my speed, allowing the rhythm of the night to soothe the edges of tension.

"Where are we going anyway?" Sienna asks. The dreadful question I was hoping to somehow avoid for the rest of my life. The truth hovers on the tip of my tongue, but the fear of her reaction holds it back. Instead, I choose my words carefully, for now.

"Somewhere safe, sweet."

CHAPTER 2:

OPERATION SKYLAR

Dean

How did I end up in this fucking mess?

I scan my eyes across the shitshow unfolding around me; a dead girl just casually bleeding out on my right, Birdie and Delilah crying to my left, coppers surrounding us. The scene could be lifted straight from a bad movie. I stand there, momentarily frozen, watching Marcus tear away on his bike, Sienna gripping onto him for dear life. A dynamic duo attempting a Houdini-like escape.

"Nice one, Marcus." I mutter sarcastically under my breath, my lips curling into a dry smirk as his audacious manoeuvre includes an unexpected scrape between the police car and his bike mirror. As he disappears into the night, I shake my head in disbelief.

I'm about to be on the run with this guy?

Turning back to Delilah, I realise the clock is ticking, and I've got a decision to make. The sirens grow louder, the flashing lights more insistent, and as one of the police cars races off behind Marcus, I'm urged to act. It's time to go. I look down at Delilah, tears and concern welling in her gorgeous, moss-green eyes as she glares back up at me.

"Are you sure you don't want to change your mind?" I ask, trying to convince her to come with me. She nods her head subtly as her bottom lip begins to quiver. "You'll be safer with me." I continue as I rub my thumb lightly across her cheek.

"My family is here." she whimpers. I give a silent nod, grasping the reasoning behind her words, and then plant a firm kiss on her forehead.

"I'll be back soon to check on you, okay? I promise."

"Be safe."

"Always, my darling."

I pivot away from Delilah, moving with purpose towards the police car where Skylar sits defiantly in the back seat; the unwilling star of this twisted performance. A wry grin etches its way onto my face as I approach. The absurdity of the situation isn't lost on me.

Her pastel pink hair glows through the window, a bizarre contrast against the stark, monochromatic backdrop of the crime scene. I chuckle to myself with an odd sense of amusement. Skylar, usually the wildcard in our escapades, has now become an unexpected protagonist.

Approaching the police car with a calculated nonchalance, I consider the best way to execute the upcoming rescue mission. A quick scan of the surroundings reveals the focus of the police officers elsewhere. Perfect. With a creak, I swing the door open, revealing Skylar's defiant gaze. Tears stream down her face in unbridled hysteria, leaving trails of smeared makeup in their wake.

"Fucking hell, you look a mess." I laugh.

"Maybe we should've let you die, prick." She snaps with a cold glare.

A little harsh.

"So, you just felt like running someone over tonight?" I tease, gripping her arm to pull her out. She reluctantly swings her legs around to step out of the car, rolling her eyes in the meantime.

"What can I say? I like to make an entrance."

The night wraps around us like a shroud as Skylar and I slip away from the tumult, our hurried footsteps echoing through the deserted alleys. We quickly begin to sprint with unbridled urgency, our legs pumping relentlessly against the pavement. The cityscape blurs around us as we cover ground with a desperate determination to put distance between us and the scene. The rhythmic pounding of our steps harmonising with the adrenaline coursing through our veins.

We need to find a car.
Now.

As we sprint through the alleys I notice Skylar starting to lag behind.

"A little bit of urgency would be nice!" I taunt.

"Yeah, okay. You try to run with your hands cuffed behind your back! It's not as easy as it looks, knobhead!"

"I have, many times!"

Finally, I spot a car parked along the curb. Relief floods through me as I approach our ticket to escape. I pull on the handle, hoping for an easy steal. No luck. Skylar eventually catches up, positioning herself on the passenger side, as I focus on the task of prying the door open. Which is pretty much impossible considering I have no fucking tools with me.

"A little bit of urgency would be nice." Skylar mocks with an arrogant smile.

"Fair play, cunt." I concede with a nod as I continue to pry at the door for a while longer, but to no avail. The urgency of the situation reverberates in my mind, a relentless reminder that time is slipping away.

"Ah, fuck it." I mutter through gritted teeth, my frustration and pressure mounting, as I smash through the window in a single punch; blood instantly spilling from my knuckles.

"Dean!" Skylar shrieks.

"You got a better idea? Huh?" I question, my voice raising "Yeah, didn't think so." I slide into the car and ping open the passenger door. "Get in the fucking car."

Without a moment's hesitation, I ignite the engine, and the vehicle surges forward onto the road, the tyres screeching as they skid against the asphalt. Skylar, still nursing her bound wrists, shoots me a sceptical glance, her eyes a cocktail of disbelief and exhilaration. The city lights streak past like shooting stars, and I begin to relax as a small weight lifts from my shoulders; alive with the thrill of escape once again.

As for Sky, well she doesn't look so relaxed. A mischievous smirk graces my lips as I crank up the car radio, filling the vehicle with a pulsating wave of sound. Her eyes burn into me as she scrunches her face in unmistakable anger.

"Turn it off!"

"Sorry, can't hear you!" I shrug. Skylar's scowl deepens, and she struggles against her restraints.

"Ugh! I'm serious! Dean, turn it off!" A devilish glint dances in my eyes as, instead, I proceed to raise the volume to the max. As the music reaches its zenith, Skylar leans closer, her voice now a determined whisper.

"Dean Douglas, if you don't turn it off right now I swear to God I'll-"

The threat remains unfinished as the road ahead suddenly transforms into a wash of blinding headlights. My reflexes kick in, and I swerve violently to avoid a head-on collision. The tyres screech in protest, and for a brief, heart-stopping moment, it feels like we're right back on the edge of disaster. Skylar's scream mingles with the abrupt silence as the near-miss unfolds.

The car narrowly avoids collision, and I exhale a breath I didn't realise I was holding.

"Fuck me, that was close." I admit with a chuckle as I turn off the radio.

"Are you fucking serious?"

"It was an accident, chill."

"Chill? You almost got us killed and you want me to fucking chill?"

"I'll gladly take you back to the police car if that's what you'd prefer?" I raise my eyebrows and look over at her.

Death glare.

She's giving me the Skylar-death-glare.

I lean back in my seat with a sigh before backing down, "Alright, alright. My bad."

"So what's your plan exactly?" Skylar asks, breaking a few minutes of silence.

"Marcus is gonna meet us at a B&B a couple hours away and we're checked in there for a few weeks."

"A few weeks?"

"Yeah, Marcus and I have some people on our backs."

"Ahh, I always knew you were a scammy dealer. That's why I never bought from you."

"How do you know I've been dealing?" Skylar rolls her eyes, a playful smirk dancing on her lips.

"Are you really asking me that? You're like the most stereotypical looking drug dealer I've ever seen."

"Ouch."

"It's the truth."

"And I'm not scammy. I'm.. strategic."

"Whatever you wanna call it.

"Back on topic," she continues, "what happens after these few weeks?"

"Yeah, our plan hasn't really gone any further than that."

"Wonderful." she says, rolling her eyes.

"We're gonna figure it out, just roll with it, Sky."

"Yeah, yeah. You're paying for my room."

CHAPTER 3:
FAR FROM HOME

Sienna

I often wonder, what cruel logic, if any, governs the arbitrary distribution of life's suffering and serenity? What cosmic lottery decides who gets calm and who gets chaos? I mean, genuinely, what on earth did I ever do to deserve all the things I have to deal with? I'm beginning to suspect that my past-life self might have been a *little* bit of a twat.

After a couple of annoyingly-secretive hours of riding, we finally arrive at a small B&B situated in the midst of nowhere. I swing my leg over and hop off the bike, determined to absorb the surroundings despite the shroud of darkness enveloping the night sky above. The only illumination emanates from the warm glow spilling through the windows of the rural building before me.

What in the world is going on?

I turn to face Marcus, fully intending to sternly demand some answers, but the moment my eyes catch him dismounting the bike, my resolve shatters. My thoughts scatter like leaves in the wind as I get lost in the details that make him, well.. him.

His dark brown hair, charmingly tousled, framing his face perfectly; while the play of shadows highlights every contour of his tall, toned body. His light, rugged facial hair outlining his jaw. The deep dimple that forms on his left cheek when he flashes me that beautiful, sick smirk.

He's the kind of man who knows how to take exactly what he wants. Which should make me nervous, of course.

Yet as his piercing hazel eyes lock onto mine and that crooked smirk plays on his lips, I instead become acutely aware of the throbbing between my legs.

He's a walking contradiction and, despite the warning bells, I can't deny the thrill that comes with the realisation that he's exactly the kind of bad, evil man that I shouldn't want. But I do.

As he steps closer, I open my mouth to speak but my words get caught in my throat as the subtle intensity in his eyes locks me into place. The curl of his lips deepening as though he's aware of the effect he has on me.

"Got something to say, sweet?" Marcus' voice, low and gravelly, sends a shiver down my spine. I swallow hard, attempting to gather my thoughts.

"Where are we?" I manage, my voice confident and triumphing over the nervous flutter in my chest.

"That's for me to know." He says, leaning in with a wink before walking past me and towards the building. "You coming?" he asks, holding the door open for me.

I take a deep breath, my mind still racing with questions, but the allure of the unknown draws me forward. With a reluctant nod, I follow him into the cosy B&B, the door closing behind us with a soft click. The interior is exactly as you'd expect from a random bed and breakfast out in the countryside; quaint, with rustic furniture and dim lighting. Marcus approaches the small front desk, its surface adorned with a weathered bell that hints at years of stories and arrivals.

He presses the bell and stares down at me as we wait for a response. His eye contact is intense. He's not looking at me, but rather he's looking into me. The intensity of his focus is both intimidating and strangely affectionate, a paradoxical mix that leaves me entranced. In those moments, he's not just staring; it's as if he's unravelling me with his eyes.

And as the seconds tick by, one single thought occupies my mind..

I want to kiss him.

Yes, I want to kiss a murderer.

Suddenly an unexpected creaking sound steals my attention. Descending a set of stairs, an elderly man in a dressing gown appears. His eyes, gentle yet perceptive, meet ours as he reaches the bottom step, and a warm smile graces his weathered face.

"Sorry for the delay. We don't usually have people arrive this late in the night." He begins. I manage a small smile, feeling a mixture of relief and embarrassment for being caught in such an obviously intimate moment.

"All good, man." Marcus responds. "I've got a booking for the next few weeks."

Weeks?

"Lovely, what name is the booking under?"
"Dean."

Dean?

My mind rolls back to the gun laying in Marcus' bag and suddenly fear overtakes my body again. My heart starts to beat harder through my chest and my vision becomes unsteady. I try to slow my breathing, my mind racing through the fragments of information Marcus has just casually shared. He notices my anxiety rising and reaches out to touch my arm, causing a conflict to erupt within me.

Despite my rising fear, part of me still craves the false-safety of the familiar. Still craves the man I grew up with, and I'm worried I always will. Somehow, even after all that he's done, he makes me feel safe.

The elderly man retrieves a set of glasses resting on the desk and gracefully slides them onto the bridge of his nose. He settles into the chair, the rhythm of clicking keys and the soft hum of his computer filling the air as he adeptly works on the keyboard.

"Okay, looks like you've got a booking for two double rooms?"

"Yeah, that's the one." Marcus confirms.

Though it irks me to admit it, my heart faintly aches at the revelation that Marcus had booked us separate rooms. Surely he would want to be in bed with me, right?

Not that I want that, of course.

"Great, follow me." With a friendly smile, he briskly escorts us back outside, making his way across a small dirt path, toward a line of five twee cottage-style outbuildings. He gestures towards the two buildings at the end of the line before handing Marcus two sets of keys. With a few parting words, the man strolls away, leaving Marcus and I alone once more.

Marcus smirks as he unlocks the door, breaking the silence settling between us.

"Come on in, beautiful." I love it when he calls me beautiful. Growing up, I never obsessed over my appearance. Never really even thought about it; there were far weightier matters to contend with, like navigating life without my parents. Sure, I knew I wasn't unattractive, but I also never considered myself particularly beautiful.

But his words, delivered with such sincerity, made me think about it more. And as I did, I began to see it too. His focus on my beauty served as a gentle mirror, revealing facets of myself I had overlooked or simply never cared to think about. I began to enjoy my beauty. And while I still don't like to dwell much on aesthetics, there's an undeniable sweetness in knowing that in his eyes, I'm the most beautiful thing in the world.

I follow him inside, the sudden warmth enveloping us. The room is surprisingly nice. Almost homely. Marcus locks the door behind us, the twist of the lock echoing through the room. Rather than placing the keys on the side, he discreetly tucks them into his back pocket, arousing my suspicion and fear once again.

As my uncertainty rises I take a few steps back, creating some distance between us. We lock eyes, both hesitant to break the silence by speaking first.

Come on Sienna, don't be such a wimp.

"You need to tell me what's going on. Right now." I assert, irritatingly-weakly.

"Curiosity killed the cat, sweet," he teases, his voice low and dripping with a seductive edge. My heartbeat quickens, partly from frustration and partly from an unsettling allure.

"I'm serious, Marcus. Tell me what's happening or I'm leaving." He leans against a rustic dresser, the subtle play of shadows accentuating the contours of his rugged features.

"But where's the fun in that?" he replies cryptically.

"Fun? You think I'm interested in having fun right now? First you confess to me that you're some kind of psycho killer, then I watch Millie die right in front of me and suddenly you're whisking me away to a cottage in the middle of nowhere and you think I care about having fun?"

The silence continues as I watch Marcus carefully consider his next words. I pose another question, aiming to simplify the clearly very complicated situation.

"Why is it booked in Dean's name?"

"Because Dean is on his way. The second room is his."

"So we're not in separate rooms?" I accidentally say out loud, far too quickly, causing Marcus to smirk even more smugly than usual.

Sienna, you absolute idiot.

He laughs softly as he takes a few steps towards me.

"No, sweet. We're not in separate rooms. I wouldn't torture you like that." I roll my eyes and cross my arms, failing to let his cocky demeanour crack me.

"Marcus, please. Just tell me what's going on."

"We're on the run, sweet. Dean's been dealing and got some dangerous people on his back. Plus the police found your little boyfriend 'Skinny Jeans' body."

Marcus sighs at my silence, his eyes searching for the right words. "Look, I didn't wanna get you tangled up in this mess. But circumstances changed, and I had to act fast."

"I'm not staying here." I scoff.

"You don't have a choice."

"Excuse me?"

"You're safe here, Sienna."

"Oh great, I'm so glad the murderer is here to teach me a lesson about safety."

"You're very cute when you're mad, my love." he says with a soft laugh.

"I'm not even your girlfriend."

"We've been over this, sweet. Put whatever label on it you want, It doesn't matter. You're mine, and I'm gonna make sure I keep you safe. Whether you like it or not."

I clench my jaw in frustration and attempt to barge past him towards the door but he softly and effortlessly pushes me back.

"I'm leaving. I mean it." I state firmly.

"Oh yeah?"

"Yes." With that, he crouches to my eye level, his gaze now stern.

"You step foot out of this room without my permission and there will be consequences. Is that clear?" Before I can formulate a response, Marcus closes the remaining distance. Our faces are inches apart, the fucked up sexual tension between us impossible to ignore.

Just as the intensity peaks, a sudden knock on the door startles us both. Marcus maintains eye contact, his authoritative expression turning into a knowing smile before he heads towards the door.

CHAPTER 4:
A SKYLAR SURPRISE

Marcus

As I swing open the door, I'm greeted with one extra pink-haired, handcuffed person than expected.

"What the fuck is she doing here?"

"Ah yes, hello to you too, Marcus." Skylar chips in sarcastically, receiving no reply. "Well, fuck you all then. I'm going to my room. Twats." With that kind comment, Skylar walks off down the dirt path and up to her room, tripping over a stone on the way.

"It's a long story." Dean mumbles, shaking his head.

"We need to talk," I start, "In your room, not here." I can't let Sienna listen, no way. It'll freak her out far too much knowing how serious this situation really is.

My sweet angel doesn't need that.

I'm painfully aware of how much I'm fucking with her anxiety just by bringing her here and it's killing me. But I have no choice. Her safety remains my top priority, no matter the circumstances.

I take a seat in Dean's room and we each roll up a joint. The smoke gradually filling the air around us.

"What on earth were you thinking bringing Sky here?" I question, entirely perplexed.

"Yeah, I'm not sure I made the right call on that one."

"You don't say." We exchange a muffled laugh. "So, what's your plan from here?"

"Lay low." Dean replies with a puff of smoke.

"That's it? Just sit still and wait? Let these cunts slowly hunt us down?"

"I don't see what else we can do?"

"Fight back. When have we ever allowed people to walk over us? We can't just sit here like pussies."

"Bro, it's not just some random kid from the estate we're fucking with. These are dangerous people, far more dangerous than us."

"Why are you even on their radar to begin with?"

Dean releases a protracted, tension-laden sigh. The palpable burden upon his shoulders becomes increasingly evident. The weight, both metaphorical and tangible, pressing down on him like an unwelcome companion, leaving an indelible mark on his posture and expression.

"That's the weirdest part." he reluctantly begins, "I'm not exactly sure. Don't get me wrong, I owe a lot of fuckers money. But these guys, not a penny."

"That makes no sense." I blurt out, scrunching up my face in total confusion. "Who are they?"

"They're all working for the same guy. Calls himself 'Grizzly'."

"Real intimidating," I chuckle sarcastically, "And you have no idea what he wants from you?"
Dean shakes his head and shrugs defeatedly.

"I can only assume they want money. We deal in the same areas but I don't see how I could possibly be any threat to their business."

We sit in speechless thought for a few moments, grappling with the situation. The hushed atmosphere is occasionally punctuated by the rhythmic sound of inhalation and exhalation as we each take deliberate puffs on our joints.

In this chill silence, our blunts aren't just rolled-up temporary escapes; they're like conversation pieces passing between us. Each puff feels like a nod of understanding, a quiet acknowledgment that we're both trying to make sense of everything being thrown our way.

"Let's find him." I eagerly suggest.

"Are you mad?"

"I mean it." Dean looks at me with a mixture of disbelief and concern, his eyes searching mine for any sign that I might be joking. "We can't just sit here and wait for trouble to arrive," I declare, exhaling a plume of smoke. "We need to take control of the situation. Find these guys before they find us."

Dean leans back in his chair, a thoughtful expression on his face. The room is filled with the pungent aroma of cannabis as our joints burn slowly, the smoke swirling around us like a protective haze.

"I get your point, bro, but these people are organised, and they've got something bigger at play. Going after them blindly could make this shit a whole lot worse," Dean warns.

Ignoring the scepticism in Dean's eyes, I lean forward, determined to drive my point home.

"Waiting around is a death sentence, man. We need to at least figure out what we're up against" Dean takes a thoughtful drag from his joint, considering my words.

"Alright, let's say we find them. What's the plan then? We can't just barge in and demand answers. It's not that simple." he rambles, "And how would we find them anyway?"

"That's where Skylar comes in," I suggest. "She's got connections. She knows just as many dealers as we do, and she's close with them. If anyone can help us navigate this mess without drawing attention, it's her." Dean raises an eyebrow, a sceptical look returning to his face.

"You trust her that much?"
I shrug.

"Not necessarily, but she's our best bet." After a brief moment of contemplation, Dean nods in agreement.

"Alright, I'll talk to Skylar." Dean begins to stand up and finishes his blunt. "We have to be careful here, bro." He warns, his face serious. "We're stepping into some deep shit, and it's not just *our* lives on the line." He tilts his head subtly in the direction of my room, a silent indication to Sienna that instantly sends a shiver down my spine.

I give a clear, understanding nod as I take a final puff. His insinuation lands like a leaden weight in my chest, stifling any words that dare to rise. Instead it creates a tangible lump in my throat. Realising that Dean believes my plan could jeopardise Sienna's safety hits me like a sledgehammer to the heart. Words fail me in this moment, not for lack of understanding, but because the depth of my sudden emotions transcends mere language.

Are we doing the right thing here?

CHAPTER 5:

HUNT FOR GRIZZLY

Dean

"I'm asleep!" Sky shouts as I knock on the door.

"For real, Skylar, I need to talk to you."

The door flings open, revealing a definitely-not-asleep Skylar with a hint of annoyance in her eyes.

"This better be good." she mutters, stepping aside to let me in.

"Oh you're gonna love it. The topic is drug dealers, your favourite."

"I fucked two drug dealers, okay? Can we just let it die?" As Skylar sits down I lean against the wall in front of her, head in hand.

"As much as I would *love* to, no. They might be able to help us out with something."

"No, no, no." Skylar begins, shaking her head and arms dramatically. "I'm sick and tired of trying to help you morons. Look at what just happened. Marcus, oh-so-simply suggests '*hey Sky, it would be really helpful if you would go get us a car*' next thing you know I've splattered Millie across the car park."

"To be fair, I don't think getting chased by feds and killing Millie was mentioned in his instructions."

Probably not the wisest response from me.

Skylar shoots me a glare that could freeze lava.

"I mean, I did pay for your room so you kinda owe me." I continue, stupidly trying my luck.

"Dean, shut the fuck up." I slowly retrieve a paperclip I had snagged from the front desk and start twirling it between my fingers.

"I guess you don't mind keeping those handcuffs on then?" I suggest with a dramatic huff. Skylar's eyes narrow at my attempt to blackmail her.

"Unlock them. Now."

"Help me. Now." There's a long pause as Skylar's eyes burn through my skin.

"Fine. What do you want?"

"I want you to message your little fuckbuddy drug dealers and ask them for some info."

"What *kind* of info?"

"Anything and everything they know about a guy who goes by Grizzly."

"Grizzly? All this chaos and we're running from a guy called Grizzly?" Skylar bursts into genuine laughter. "Is he friends with the big bad wolf or some shit?"

"Hilarious.. So, are you gonna help?"
Skylar's laughter gradually subsides as she regains her composure, blinking away a tear from her eye.

"Okay, okay. I'll message them and see what I can dig up. Just please, for the love of all that's holy, unlock me now."

With steady hands, I carefully insert the paperclip into the lock, recalling the lessons I learned from watching Skylar do the same countless times before. The mechanism clicks softly as I apply gentle pressure, and with a sense of triumph, the handcuffs spring open. Skylar rubs her wrists with a sigh of relief, the tension in the room easing as the metal restraints fall away. There's actually a moment of quiet gratitude between us.

Wholesome friendship.

"Thanks, twat."

Nevermind.

As Skylar picks up her phone to send the messages, I take a step back, giving her some space to work her magic.

"Do they usually reply fast?" I ask.

"Depends. Sometimes they answer straight away, sometimes they leave me hanging."

"You know, Sky, at this hour? They'll probably reply instantly in hopes they're gonna get a little more than just a sale."

"Very funny."

"I'm serious."

"We don't just hook up, okay? We have a good relationship." She insists, trying to convince herself.

"Aww, do they bring you flowers when they come to rail you and drop off your drugs?" Skylar rolls her eyes as she tries to hold in her escaping laughter.

"Sadly not everyone can have what you and Delilah have."

"You deserve more though." As Skylar shoots me a sidelong glance, there's a flicker of vulnerability in her expression, a hint of longing hidden beneath her tough exterior. It's a rare glimpse into the softer side of her, a side that she guards fiercely.

"But the kind of love you and Delilah share.. It's like something out of a fairy tale. It's rare, Dean. It's not the kind of love most people get to experience. Definitely not somebody like me. I'm too broken. No normal, good guy is ever gonna deal with my baggage."

"Then that's not a *good* guy." I reply, my voice firm and resolute. "No good guy would see your past as 'baggage'. It's not baggage, Sky, it's your story. Don't ever let what we went through make you question your ability to be loved."

Skylar's glare meets mine and a begrudged smile flickers across her lips. Behind that forced smile lies an obvious shadow of doubt that tugs at my heartstrings a little. It's as if she doesn't believe me, doesn't believe that she deserves the kind of love I'm talking about. As strange as it is for me to say, I actually feel bad for her.

As I begin to make my way to the door, I offer Skylar a reassuring smile, my hand reaching out to grasp the handle.

"Let me know if you hear anything, yeah?"

"Will do." With a nod, I slowly step out, gently closing the door behind me.

The cool night air greets me, and I fish out a cigarette, lighting it with practised ease before embarking on a leisurely stroll toward my own cottage situated at the end of the row. Each step is deliberate, allowing me to mull over the evening's events as the smoke curls lazily around me. The night is quiet, except for the occasional rustle of leaves and distant hoot of an owl.

As I reach my room, lost in thought, a sudden crack splits the silence, followed by the sound of splintering wood. My instincts kick in, and I barely have time to react before a massive tree limb crashes down from above, landing with a deafening thud just a few feet away from me.

What the fuck just happened?
I can't help but gape at the sight of the fallen limb, utterly dumbfounded. The night was calm, no hint of any strong wind, yet here I am, staring at a tree branch that decided to take a nosedive out of nowhere. I scratch my head, trying to wrap my mind around the bizarre occurrence. It's like the universe decided to play a prank on me, except this isn't the kind of joke I find funny.

Glancing around, I half-expect to see hidden cameras, waiting for my reaction. But there's nothing. Just the usual quiet of the night, broken only by the rustle of leaves in the gentle breeze. It's as if the world is shrugging its shoulders, just as clueless about what just happened as I am.

With a furrowed brow, I turn my attention back to the fallen limb, its presence casting a long shadow across the ground. I crouch down beside it, running my fingers along its rough surface, trying to glean some insight into its sudden descent.

But the limb remains stubbornly silent, offering no answers. I stub out my cigarette, the ember fizzling out in the darkness, and I make my way back inside, leaving the fallen limb behind me. Whatever caused it to fall, I'm not in the mood to figure it out tonight.

CHAPTER 6:
WHO'S IN CHARGE?

Sienna

Marcus reenters the room; the unmistakable scent of marijuana following him. He immediately buries the keys in his pocket and confronts me with that sick, tempting smile.

Remember, you're angry Sienna! You're really really angry.

I stand up off the bed and face him, arms folded tightly across my chest.

"Why are you still awake, beautiful? You must be exhausted." he begins, his words laced with a charm that threatens to disarm my anger.

"Take me home."

"I am your home." he counters softly.

"Marcus, you can't keep me here. This is like.. kidnapping." He chuckles darkly, taking a deliberate step closer.

"Kidnapping implies you're not here willingly, sweet. And we both know that's not the case." His words are like a punch to the gut, leaving me breathless and uncertain. I know he's right in a twisted sort of way. My pulse quickens at the reminder of just how deeply entangled I've become in his web.

He strides towards me, his presence commanding and dominating, until he stands towering over me, casting a shadow that seems to engulf my entire being.

"I'm trying to keep you safe."

"Keep me safe? Really? By trapping me here against my will?" I question, "Give me the keys, Marcus. Now." His gaze hardens, his eyes flashing with possessive determination.

"You want the keys?" He taunts with a smirk, his voice laced with amusement as he takes a seat on the edge of the bed. With a brazen display of confidence, he slips them down into the front of his pants, his eyes never leaving mine. "Take 'em."

A rush of conflicting emotions washes over me; anger, frustration, and a hint of something else which I dare not acknowledge.

"I'm not playing games. I want to go home."

"You're making this so much worse for yourself."

"Do you seriously think you can just keep me here?"

"I can and I will." He asserts, his tone laced with a chilling certainty. "I'm doing what I need to do to keep you safe. You have no choice in this."

"I'll find a way out, sooner or later."

"Oh yeah?" He raises an eyebrow, "Then what? You don't even know where we are, sweet."

"I'll figure it out." Marcus' smirk widens, his amusement evident as he leans back against the bed, his posture relaxed yet oozing with dominance.

"You're pushing your luck now." Marcus starts after a short silence, "Please, let's just get some sleep." he suggests, before standing up and pulling back the duvet for me with a gentle tug.

"Fine, but don't expect me to still be here when you wake up." I threaten with venom, and almost instantly regret.

His jaw tightens, and his eyes narrow with a predatory focus I've never seen before. He immediately paces towards me, closing the distance until we're face to face; his eyes ablaze with fury as he crouches down to my eye level, our gazes locked in a tense standoff.

"I fucking dare you." For a moment, silence reigns, broken only by the sound of our shallow breaths filling the space between us. "Try to sneak out and watch what happens."

"What are you gonna do? You gonna kill me too?" I challenge, trying to keep my voice steady despite the tremble in my limbs. "I'm not scared of you."

"I don't want you to be scared of me. I want you to respect my orders."

"Or what?" I ask spitefully, as I push my face even closer to his, daring him to respond.

Bad idea.

In one sharp motion he grabs me by the throat and forcefully pins me against the wall. His mixed scent of aftershave and weed overtaking my senses.

"Let me make myself fucking clear, sweet. You leave this room and you'll be punished until I think you've learnt your lesson."

"Punished?" I manage to choke out, my voice strained under his relentless grip.

"Yes, pretty. Punished." Marcus' grip tightens, his fingers digging into my flesh with cruel intensity. "I'll have my way with you until you're crying out for mercy. Begging me to stop."

I know, I know. I should be terrified. But right now looking up into those hazel-green eyes, *all* I want is whatever he's thinking about doing to me. Every single dirty, twisted, painful fantasy he has going on in that insane mind. I want it all.

"You're a sick, sadistic-." My sentence is cut off by his grip somehow still tightening around my throat.

"Are you sure you want to continue that sentence?" he asks in a deep whisper.

Tears prickle at the corners of my eyes as I struggle to breathe, the world spinning around me. With all the strength I can muster, I somehow manage to shake my head. Marcus' grip tightens for a moment longer before, with a sudden jolt, he releases me. I stagger backward, my legs giving way beneath me, and I collapse to my knees, gasping for air.

Marcus slowly crouches down in front of me, his gorgeous, vein covered hand firm as it grips my chin, forcing me to look at him.

"Look at me, sweet." he commands calmly, "As much as I'd enjoy disciplining you, I'd prefer you didn't give me a reason to." His grip on my chin tightens, his fingers pressing into my skin with an uncomfortable force leaving bruises blossoming beneath his touch. "Have I made myself clear?"

"I don't even have any clothes here," the words escape me in a feeble attempt to divert the conversation, to cling to some semblance of normalcy. But even as the words leave my lips, I know they're futile. His gaze narrows, and for a moment, I catch a flicker of something unreadable in his expression before it softens, just barely. It's a small reprieve, a fleeting moment of tenderness.

"I'll take care of that." He promises, his voice a low rumble.

As he reaches out to touch my cheek, a shiver runs down my spine, a chill that cuts through the warmth of his touch. I know I should pull away, should resist the temptation of his embrace, but I find myself leaning into his touch. Marcus rises to his feet and begins looking through his bag as I stay frozen on the floor. He pulls out one of his black t-shirts and returns to where I'm kneeling, gently crouching down to offer it to me.

"Wear this for tonight." he says softly, his voice barely above a whisper, yet it resonates with an undeniable authority. It's a command disguised as a suggestion, leaving me with little choice but to comply.

I take off my top to change, revealing my bare chest. As Marcus watches me, I can see the hint of a smile playing at the corners of his lips, a subtle satisfaction in knowing that he has me under his control. It's both infuriating and extremely fucking attractive, a constant tug-of-war.

"So pretty." he states, his eyes devouring me hungrily.

I slide his t-shirt over my head and enjoy the feeling of his aroma engulfing me. It's like I'm wrapping myself in him.

"There you go. Good girl." he murmurs, his voice laced with approval.

I sit in his oversized t-shirt, as he watches me intently, his eyes lingering on every movement as if he's savouring the moment.

"Are you happy now?" I snap, with a smirk of my own. Marcus' expression remains unreadable for a moment before a thick smile curls his lips.

"You have no idea how happy I am, seeing you in that."

I begin to stand up but before I can even reach my feet, Marcus moves with lightning speed, effortlessly scooping me up over his shoulder.

"Marcus, put me down!" I protest, my fists pounding against his back in a pathetic 'attempt' to break free. But Marcus pays no heed, his grip firm as he carries me towards the bed.

Just as I'm about to unleash another barrage of complaints, I feel a hard, sharp smack to my ass that sends a jolt of surprise and pain coursing through me.

"Hey!" I start, indignation rising in my throat, but Marcus cuts me off with a playful chuckle.

"Consider that another reminder of who's in charge."

In one swift motion, he slams me onto the mattress, the force of it knocking the wind out of me. Before I can even gather my wits, he's straddling me, pinning me down; one hand still lingering on my now tingling backside. Despite myself, a blush creeps across my cheeks.

"I love when you give me attitude, sweet. It really fucking turns me on. But sometimes you have to relax and stop fighting me." he chides, his fingers tracing lazy circles on my skin. Despite my best efforts to resist, a shiver runs down my spine at his touch.

It's not fair for him to be this hot.

Before I can faux-protest and further, his fingers dig into my sides, eliciting a squeal of laughter as he tickles me mercilessly. I squirm and wriggle beneath him, unable to contain the infectious giggles that bubble up from deep within me.

Just as quickly as it began, Marcus relents, his touch softening into gentle caresses as he peppers slow, firm kisses all over my body. I catch my breath, my laughter fading into contented sighs and whimpers. It's a dizzying whirlwind of sensations, leaving me breathless and disoriented.

"Now," he starts, whispering in between kisses, "are you gonna get some sleep?"

I nod, my eyelids heavy with the promise of much-needed rest. Marcus's lips trail down my neck, leaving a tingling sensation in their wake as he murmurs, "Very smart."

"Sleep tight, sweet."

CHAPTER 7:
ONE STEP CLOSER

Dean

I bang on Marcus' door as I start rolling my first joint of the day. the crinkling sound of the paper and the sweet aroma of freshly ground cannabis waft up. The door swings open, and Marcus emerges with a brisk step, swiftly slamming it shut behind him. He takes one look at me and my blunt and lets out a huff.

"What's the issue?" I ask, knowing exactly what the issue is.

"It's not even 10 a.m."

"I deserve an early joint after gathering info all night."

"Sure, keep telling yourself that." We both settle into my stolen car and I start the engine with a loud rumble.

"So, what have you got for me?" he asks,

"I had Sky message her little druggy friends and they actually had some info on one of Grizzly's runners." I say, handing him the joint. Marcus takes a long drag, his eyes squinting against the smoke.

"Nice, do share." he says, passing the joint back to me.

"This guy goes by the name of Razor. Apparently, he's been moving some serious weight lately, and he's got ties to Grizzly. If we can track him down, we might get some leads on where he's been hiding." Marcus nods, his mind already churning.

"So where do we find this guy?"

"There's a rundown warehouse about an hour away. Word is, that's where he operates out of. I figure we pay him a visit, see if he's willing to talk."

"Sounds like a plan," Marcus says, a glint of determination in his eyes. "Let's go pay Razor a visit."

As we approach, the areas become increasingly gloomy, graffiti-covered walls and broken windows decorating the landscape. Feels just like home.

I fucking love it.

"Shit." Marcus mutters under his breath as he stares at his phone screen.

"What's up?"

"They're expanding the search for the murder." he explains. I shrug.

"So? They're not gonna find you where we're staying."

"I hope you're right." he sighs, rubbing his head.

As we pull up to the warehouse, I reach behind me, my hand finding the familiar bulk of the bag nestled in the backseat. With practised ease, I withdraw my gun, it's cold steel fitting snugly into my palm like a well-worn glove. A quick glance at Marcus confirms his readiness, his nod signalling the presence of his own weapon, snug in his waistband. A grin spreads across his face, reminiscent of the mischief we used to get up to as kids, and for a moment, the tension of the impending confrontation is broken by a shared memory of simpler times.

"Remember the time we broke into that abandoned factory and got into a fight?" I ask with a smile. Marcus's expression falters, and for a moment, I can almost see the memory unfold in his mind.

"How could I forget? We were lucky to make it out alive." he says, a low laugh rumbling up.

"Yeah, we had a few bruises to explain to the home staff." Marcus nods, a wistful look creeping over his face.

"Those were the days."

"We were trouble."

"Some things never change." With that we turn to each other, sharing a knowing glance. I slide my gun into my waistband, feeling its weight against my hip.

"You ready?" He asks.

"Let's fucking go." With a shared nod, we simultaneously open the car doors and step out.

Razor doesn't know what's coming.

The gravel crunches beneath us as we approach the worn, corrugated steel door. The faded sign creaks in the gentle breeze, reading 'Industrial Warehouse' in rusty letters. We exchange a look, and then, together, we push the creaking door open, revealing the musty interior. The silence is a palpable thing, punctuated only by the hollow echo of our footsteps as we step into the cavernous space.

Adrenaline courses through my veins as we venture deeper into the heart of the building, every sense heightened, every nerve on edge. The only sounds are the faint echoes of our footsteps, resonating off the walls in a rhythmic cadence, punctuated by the occasional drop of water from a leaking pipe. Then, without warning, a voice pierces the silence, sharp and commanding, making me jump slightly.

"Who the fuck is in here?"

We press on, moving deeper into the labyrinthine space. As we round a corner we come face to face with what has to be Razor, considering the large tattoo of a razor blade across his throat, and two other guys; a motley assortment of rough-looking characters. Razor himself stands at the forefront, a short but menacing figure.

"Well, well, well. Who do we have here?" Razor sneers, his voice dripping with contempt. "Mr. Dean Douglas, huh? What the fuck do you want?"

"We're looking for Grizzly." I start.

"And he's looking for you. Word on the street is, he's not too happy. There's a big reward out for whoever brings you to him." As Razor's smirk widens, it becomes evident that he's not about to make this easy for us.

"Where is he?" Marcus asks.

"You two think you can waltz in here and make demands?" He takes another step closer, his hand tightening into a fist. "You got balls, I'll give you that."

Marcus tenses beside me, his hand inching closer to his gun. I shoot him a warning glance, silently urging him to hold back for now.

"We're not here to start trouble," I say, keeping my tone even despite the adrenaline coursing through me. "But we need to find Grizzly. Help us, and maybe we can all walk away from this in one piece."

Razor's lips curl into a sneer, his eyes narrowing as he considers our proposal. For a moment, the only sound in the warehouse is the distant hum of traffic outside. Finally, Razor breaks the silence with a derisive laugh.

"Oh don't worry. I'll take you to Grizzly." he starts, "In a fucking bodybag. Do you know how much money I'm about to make for this?"

"It doesn't have to be like this, man. Let's talk it out." I suggest.

Suddenly, one of Razor's cronies makes a move, reaching for his gun with lightning speed. Instinct kicks in, and Marcus and I draw our weapons in unison, the sharp crack of gunfire echoing through the warehouse. In the moments that follow, bullets fly and bodies fall, the air thick with the acrid scent of gunpowder. Adrenaline courses through my veins as I take aim, my focus laser-sharp despite the chaos unfolding around me.

When the gunfire finally ceases, the warehouse is eerily silent once more, the only sound the ragged tone of our breaths. Marcus and I exchange a grim glance, our hearts pounding in our chests as we take in the aftermath of the confrontation. Razor lies on the ground, clutching a wound in his shoulder, his eyes wide with shock and pain. His two companions are sprawled motionless nearby.

With a deep breath, I crouch and hold my gun to Razor's tiny, square head.

"You've got one more fucking chance," I say, my voice low and dangerous. "Tell us where he is, or you'll end up like your friends here."

"I-I don't know where he is, okay? We're not allowed to know his location."

"Bullshit." Marcus adds.

"I'm not lying, man. I can g-give you money instead?" I push the gun harder against his temple.

"We don't want your mon-"

"How much?" I interject. Marcus gives me a confused look but I keep my eyes on Razor.

"I got a couple bags in the safe back there."

"What's the code?"

"1403." I tilt my head slightly, prompting Marcus to check the safe.

Marcus wastes no time, swiftly moving towards the safe with a sense of urgency. He punches in the code, 1403, and with a satisfying click the safe door swings open. Marcus grabs a few handfuls of cash, stuffing them into his waistband. Meanwhile, I keep my gun trained on Razor, my finger twitching on the trigger.

I stand up over him, my gun frozen in place.

"Appreciate the money, but we have a little problem, Razor." I start with a grin, "I have a terrible feeling that you're fucking lying to me." Razor's eyes widen in panic as he realises that his attempt to buy his way out of trouble has failed. Sweat beads on his forehead, and his breath comes in short, ragged gasps as he struggles to come up with a response.

"Fuck, man. I swear."

But I'm not convinced.

With a cold glint in my eyes, I press the gun harder against his temple, the metal biting into his skin.

"You expect us to believe this bullshit?" I growl, my voice low and dangerous. "You expect us to believe that Grizzly doesn't trust his own men with his location? That he doesn't have someone like you keeping tabs on his operations?"

Razor's eyes dart between us, his breathing growing more frantic with each passing second. It's clear that he's caught between a rock and a hard place, torn between the fear of crossing Grizzly and the fear of what we might do to him if he doesn't cooperate.

"I don't know where he is, I swear."

"Then you know somebody who does." Marcus adds. Razor's eyes widen in fear at my words, and I can see the wheels turning in his head as he weighs his options. He knows that we're not messing around, but he's also smart enough to know that crossing Grizzly is a death sentence.

"Fuck, fuck okay. Fine." he strains, "I-I know someone who might know. But you didn't hear it from me." I nod, satisfied that we're finally getting somewhere.

"Who is it?" I demand, my voice hard and uncompromising.

"His name's Moth."

"Where do we find him?"

"He's in London."

"Home shit home." Marcus inserts. Razor then reluctantly reveals Moth's exact whereabouts. I exchange a glance with Marcus and we share a brief, unspoken understanding that our mission is done, and it's time to exit this precarious situation.

Or so I thought.

Slowly, I take a step back, allowing Razor to untense. I tuck my gun away, ready to turn around and leave the warehouse's dark recesses behind. Marcus, however, seems to have other plans.

As I turn to make my exit, I hear a sudden gunshot ring out and Razor's skull hitting the ground. I whirl my gaze back and forth between Razor's lifeless body and Marcus, dumbfounded, trying to process what just happened.

"What the fuck was that for?" I ask. Marcus shrugs nonchalantly, as if he didn't just murder someone.

"I didn't like him."

I shake my head, trying to wrap my mind around Marcus's bizarre logic and find some words.

"I- Seriously?"

"What? He got on my nerves. You gonna miss him or something?"

I can't help but chuckle, despite the absurdity of the situation. "I'm not saying that. But did you have to shoot him right when we were about to leave?"

"Eh, it felt like the right moment."

"You know, most people just say goodbye or something." Marcus gives me a lopsided grin.

"Yeah, well, I've never been one for formalities."

"So is murder just your thing now?"

"Keeping things interesting." I rub my forehead and sigh. "Well, we've got what we came for. Let's get out of here."

"Hold on." I make my way towards a sleek black M4 parked in the corner of the warehouse.

"Nice." Marcus remarks.

"Fuck our car, I'm having this." I check the trolley next to the car and find the keys nestled on top.

Fucking morons.

"Okay, *now* let's get out of here."

CHAPTER 8:

A FRIENDLY BREAK-IN

Marcus

We get back into the car and start heading back to our rooms, but I'm not ready to go back quite yet.

"I need to make a little stop." I declare.

"Oh yeah? Where you wanna go?"

"Sienna's. I wanna grab some of her stuff."

"You got a key?" He asks.

"Nah. Smart girl knows if she ever gave me a key, I would've been barging in on her every chance I got." With a shared laugh, Dean veers towards Sienna's place.

"How you planning on doing this then?" Dean asks, curiosity gleaming in his eyes.

"I've gone in through her bedroom window before," I explain. "I'm just gonna climb in and fill a bag."

"Well, good luck with that. Since we're here, I may as well go give Delilah a visit, right?"

We pull up to the house and I hop out of the car, snatching a duffel bag from the back seat. With an obnoxious rev and wheel spin Dean shoots off into the late afternoon sunlight, leaving me to tackle my mission alone. The late afternoon sun casts a warm glow over the street, bathing the scene in a kaleidoscope of pink and orange hues. The branches of the trees stretch towards the sky, their leaves filtering the sunlight and casting intricate patterns of golden light across the pavement as I approach Sienna's window.

I glance vaguely up to the window, taking in the height as I mentally calculate the distance. With a swift burst of energy, I take a small run up and sprint towards the wall, my hands already grasping for the rough bricks as I launch myself up. The abrasive texture of the masonry scrapes against my palms as I climb.

With a grunt of effort, I reach the window ledge, fingers locking onto the frame with a vice-like grip. I continue to hold on with one arm and pry the window open with the other, the hinges protesting with a faint squeal. In a calculated motion, I propel myself upwards and into the room, landing with a purposely soft thud on the floor below.

Once inside, I take a moment to let the familiar surroundings sink in. Sienna's room is a haven of comfort, a reflection of her sweetness. Everywhere I look, there are touches of her warmth and affection. A riot of neutral and pastel colours, an abundance of teddies, plants galore and a fluffy pink cat tree. Blankets are strewn haphazardly across the bed, inviting and comforting in their disarray. The walls adorned with photographs, suncatchers casting rainbows across the room, and shelves overflowing with books; the very essence of her passions.

Her scent lingers in the air, a delicate mix of vanilla and sandalwood, calming me instantly.

I begin grabbing her clothes from the wardrobe and drawers. Every piece of clothing I handle is immaculately kept, carrying the scent of freshly laundered fabric softener. I marvel at the dainty size of each item in my hands, except for her adorably oversized jumpers that even I could practically swim in.

God, she looks so fucking sexy in those.

They make her seem so innocent, so pure, but I know better. I know the secret fire that burns beneath that soft exterior. The way she smiled as I gripped her throat on that motorbike.

Those damn jumpers, they fuck with my head, just like she does. So fucking adorable. But they hide her, and all I want to do is strip them off and show her she can't fucking hide from me. Show her just how much she drives me crazy. I imagine running my hands over her body, feeling the tremble of anticipation beneath my fingertips as she fights me verbally, yet arches against me, hungry for more. It's a fantasy I've played out a thousand times, each time more vivid than the last.

With deliberate care, I fold the clothes, taking pains to preserve them. As I finish packing, my eyes drift to the untouched bag of books in the corner; the ones I gave her just days ago. Untouched. The unopened pages seem to mock me, a tangible reminder of my haste and disregard. I curse under my breath, feeling a pang of regret for upending her life like this. Before I made the decision to change our lives.

I grab the bag of books with determination. Those books were meant for her, and she fucking deserves them, even if everything else has gone to shit. It's a small gesture, hopefully a reminder that I'm not a complete monster, despite what she might think at the moment.

As I sling the bag over my shoulder alongside the duffel, a sense of remorse washes over me. It's not often that I find myself second-guessing my actions, but at this moment, I can't shake the feeling that I've fucked her up too much. Maybe it's the way her room feels so empty without her, or maybe it's just the realisation of what I'm doing sinking in. Either way, it's not a feeling I'm used to, and it's one I'd rather not linger on.

I slip back out the window and tread down the familiar road, which is when it actually dawns on me that Dean has gone to see Delilah.

I'm gonna be waiting here for a long fucking time.

CHAPTER 9:
ALONE TIME

Dean

As my gorgeous Delilah opens the door, her lips part in a soft gasp. I'm sure she wasn't expecting to see me so soon.

"What are you doing here?" She asks with a squeal and a beaming smile.

"I'm here to see my girl, of course." I start, lifting her up. "We had some shit we needed to do a few roads up so I thought I'd pay you a visit." I carry her into the living room, planting kisses on her cheeks and forehead.

As our lips connect, there's an intense urgency in the way our hands clutch each other. Our hands begin to roam each other naturally, and fingers dig into skin.

Our kisses are fierce, hungry, as if we're trying to devour each other whole. There's no room for softness here, no matter how delicate she is.

Just as things start to heat up, and our hands start exploring more daring territories, there's a sudden interruption. From the doorway comes an audible gag, followed by Birdie's unmistakable voice.

"Ew, get a room." To which I respond plainly.

"Actually, this is a room, that had a door, that was closed."

"So sorry, Dean. I wasn't aware that I was entering your love nest, I must've mistaken it for the living room." I roll my eyes at Birdie before turning my attention back to Delilah, who is trying her best to stifle her laughter.

"I'm guessing you've filled her in on everything." I start, but before Delilah has the time to reply, Birdie answers for me.

"Yes, Dean. I know all about it. I'm glad Sky warned me never to buy from you."

"Hold on-"

"Always knew you were a dodgy dealer."

"I'm not a dodgy dealer-"

"So can I watch TV or are you guys still planning on fondling each other in here?"

With a playful glint in her eyes, Delilah takes my hand and leads me towards the staircase.

"Let's go upstairs," she suggests, her voice dropping to a sultry whisper.

As we reach her bedroom our kisses continue, intensifying by the second. I grip and caress her body with eager hands, feeling the heat radiating off her skin as she pulls me closer, her nails digging into my back. But just as things start to escalate, Delilah suddenly pulls back, her breath coming in ragged gasps.

"Wait," she murmurs, her voice husky with desire. "I almost forgot." I watch, slightly dazed, as she reaches over to her dresser, retrieving a burner phone. With a swift motion, she places it in my hand, her fingers lingering against mine for a moment longer than necessary. "Here," she says, her eyes wide and loving, "So you can stay in contact, okay?"

I nod, barely able to form coherent words as the heat between us intensifies.

"Good idea, baby." Without wasting another moment, our lips crash together once more, hungry and insatiable.

I sit on the edge of the bed and pull her straddled onto my lap. She grinds slowly against me as I suck and nibble on her neck, my hands pressed against the small of her back.

"So fucking sexy." I whisper into her ear. I tug gently on her top and continue, "Take this off for me."

Delilah complies, her movements fluid and graceful as she reveals her body for me.

I drink in the sight of her, utterly captivated by her beauty. I rub my face, attempting to conceal the elated smile that threatens to escape, and my eyes linger on hers.

"Fuck. I'm a lucky man, Delilah." Leaning in, I gently take one of her nipples into my mouth, sucking and nibbling on it lightly. Delilah lets out a soft moan, her hands coming up to run through my hair, guiding me. As I move from one breast to the other, I leave a trail of hickeys across her delicate skin. I can feel her heart pounding from beneath as I claim her.

With a breathless sigh, Delilah breaks away, her eyes dark with desire as she meets my gaze.

"Your turn," she whispers with a giggle, tugging on my shirt.

She's the cutest fucking thing on the planet.

I smirk as I discard my own shirt with a swift motion, revealing the contours of my chest and my awful self-drawn tattoos hiding beneath the fabric. Delilah's eyes widen with appreciation as she takes in the sight before her, her fingers tracing the lines of my muscles with gentle reverence.

Unable to resist any longer, I darken my eyes.

"On your knees, baby." I instruct, my voice low and commanding. Delilah's eyes sparkle with a mix of desire and anticipation as she obeys my command, her body gracefully lowering to the ground. Just the sight of her on her knees is enough to finish me off. Her eyes travel down my body, taking in the sight of me, and I can see the hunger in her eyes. I grip her chin and pull her gaze up to meet mine.

"Show me how bad you want it." I demand. Delilah's hands shake slightly as she takes me out, her eyes never leaving mine. After a few moments, she reveals the full extent of my desire for her, my arousal standing proud.

"Such a good girl." She leans forward, her tongue darting out to trace the outline of my length. With a soft moan, she takes me into her mouth, her lips wrapped around me, her tongue swirling around my shaft. I grasp her hair, my fingers gently guiding her movements, my breath hitching as she takes me deeper.

"That's it, baby. Just like that." I encourage. Delilah's response is to redouble her efforts, her tongue flicking against my most sensitive spots as her lips move in rhythm.

Every sensation becomes magnified, sending waves of pleasure coursing through my body. Her tongue dances along my length with a skill that drives me wild, her mouth a haven of ecstasy as she takes me deeper, her lips tight around me. I can feel the tension coiling within me, the anticipation of release growing stronger with each passing moment.

"Fuck."

Feeling the time is right, I gently release her from her position on her knees, guiding her to stand. As she does, I take a moment to appreciate the sight of her body before me. She's a work of fucking art.

"You've earned this, my darling." I whisper. I lay her down on the bed, positioning myself between her legs. Swiftly, her shorts and knickers are removed, and I drop them to the floor beside me.

Leaning in, I gently pin her arms above her head as I enter her.

"God, Delilah. You're so wet."

"I know." She moans softly beneath me as she bites her lip. Her hips bucking slightly as I begin to move within her. Delilah's moans grow louder, more fervent, her breaths coming in short, sharp gasps. Her body undulates, her breasts bouncing with each thrust, her nipples hardening into small, erect peaks.

"Harder." She whimpers. With a growl, I oblige to my girl's demands, thrusting deeper into her pussy, our bodies now moving in perfect harmony; every muscle, every nerve, every fibre.

"Holy fuck-" she cries out, her nails digging into my back.

"You like that, baby? You like the way I fuck that little pussy? Tell me how much you fucking like it."

I feel her walls clenching around me, urging me on, pushing me to the brink of madness. With each thrust, I can sense her release drawing nearer, and it ignites a fierce hunger within me. I drive into her relentlessly, the sound of our bodies colliding fills the room. Her eyes roll back in her head, pleasure coursing through her veins like wildfire.

"Use your words."

"Dean, I'm gonna-" she pants, her words barely coherent amidst her pleasure.

"Good. Come for me." Delilah's body tenses beneath me, her nails digging into my back as she rides the waves of pleasure crashing over her. Her moans grow louder, more urgent, as she approaches the peak of ecstasy.

"You're taking it so well, baby." I whisper with a smirk. With a primal cry, she shatters, her release cascading. I feel her walls pulsating around me, draining me for all I'm worth. "Fuck, Delilah."

As I feel Delilah's climax enveloping her, I surrender to the mounting pressure within me. With a primal roar, I spill into her, our essences mingling in a frenzy of lust.

As our panting breaths begin to slow, I kiss and caress her body, a smirk stuck arrogantly on my lips. Delilah lies there, with the body of a goddess; her skin glistening with sweat.

"I'm so proud of you." I whisper, my voice low and gravelly in her ear. "I could live inside that fucking pussy." I press a lingering kiss to her neck, my hands roaming over her trembling form. With a playful grin, I continue, "I bet you could take more too, couldn't you? My dirty little girl." She nods subtly, her eyes heavy.

"I love you." she whispers. I place a firm kiss on her temple before standing up.

"I love you more." Her eyes flutter shut and a cheesy smile takes over my face. "Looks like somebody's tired." I play.

With delicate care, I clean Delilah up, my fingertips tracing the contours of her skin with tender precision. As I dress her in a soft, buttery yellow nightgown, the fabric whispers sweet nothings against her curves, moulding itself to her form like a gentle lover as I slide it over her body.

Once she's freshened up, I move to the window and draw the curtains closed, dimming the room to create a tranquil atmosphere. The soft, diffused light casts a warm glow over Delilah's form as I turn my attention back to her.

As I step back to survey my handiwork, the room now cloaked in darkness, I notice her childhood teddy bear sitting on the bedside table. Her Grandmother had bought it for her as a kid. I remember it being practically glued to her hand when we were in the home. With a warm smile, I pick him up and place him gently in Delilah's arms.

"Our old friend." I say softly, a tender smile gracing my lips. "He'll watch over you while I'm gone. Isn't that right mate?" I pretend to ask her little friend. She laughs sleepily as I brush a stray lock of hair away from her face, tucking it behind her ear.

Before I leave, I pull a fluffy blanket from the foot of the bed and carefully drape it over her. I take a moment to ensure it's positioned just right; cocooning her properly.

"Be safe." she murmurs.

"Always." With a final tender kiss pressed to her forehead, I watch over her for a moment longer. Then, with a lingering glance, I quietly slip out of the room, leaving Delilah to drift off into dreams, knowing she's safe, satisfied and cherished.

As she *always* fucking should be.

CHAPTER 10:
SWEETS

Sienna

The door pounds open, which means that Marcus is finally back. I quickly turn away from the door to fix my hair and reapply a subtle layer of lip gloss.

God he makes me so nervous.

How do I handle myself? Attitude? Silent treatment? Kiss him? *No Sienna, you idiot.*

"Where have you been?" I snap. He doesn't respond, instead he shoots me a cold glare and a faint smile, dropping several bags in front of his feet, unzipping the big black duffel that was previously holding a gun.

"Take a guess." he says calmly, his tone betraying nothing.

My eyes flicker down to the bags, and I notice with a mixture of surprise and confusion that the duffel is filled with my clothes, neatly folded; while beside it sits the bag of books he had bought for me. The unexpected sight strikes me dumb, my ire momentarily tempered by a mix of fascination and a flicker of appreciation, as if my anger's fiery passion has been doused by the cool waters of curiosity.

"You went to get my stuff?" I ask softly.

"I told you I'd take care of it, didn't I?" he responds, his words laced with a hint of arrogance. I bristle at his tone, torn between gratitude and resentment at his control over me. Despite the gesture, I can't forget the truth of our situation. Yes, Marcus may have brought me my belongings, but I'm still his captive.

"You could have just let me leave, you know. It would've been a lot easier for both of us." I fire back, a trace of defiance seeping into my tone, and Marcus' laughter follows, a low, husky sound that sends a thrill coursing through me as he steps to the side. His eyes flicker between the door and I, a calculating glint in their depths, before settling back on me with a subtle intensity.

"The door's unlocked right now, sweet. Go ahead and leave," he challenges, his eyes locking onto mine with an intensity that makes my heart race. I hesitate, the weight of his words pressing down on me. Despite the opportunity before me, a part of me is reluctant to seize it. Deep down, I know that I'm drawn to him in ways I can't explain.

So I stand there. I just stand there.

"Changed your mind, huh?" he taunts, raising an eyebrow knowingly. I say nothing. What is there to say? He has me exactly where he wants me and honestly, I'm more than happy to be here.

Before I can respond, he locks the door behind him with a deliberate slowness. I watch him warily as he reaches into one of the bags, withdrawing a small packet of love heart sweets. His actions are calculated and the truth is I'm struggling to keep up.

With a playful grin, Marcus takes a few more steps toward me, the distance between us narrowing with each deliberate stride. He opens the bag of sweets and shakes them lightly.

"Come here," he commands, his tone firm yet strangely enticing. I obey with little hesitation, drawn to him like a moth to a flame. As I stand before him, my pulse racing madly, Marcus reaches out to take hold of my chin, tilting my head back slightly.

"Now, open your mouth," he instructs, his voice a terrifying whisper. I hesitate once more, gulping nervously as I look up at him.

"Open, Sienna. Tongue out." I comply, parting my lips as Marcus places a single sweet on my tongue. I hold my breath, waiting for his next move. My heart is racing so swiftly that I can barely catch my breath. It's as though it's attempting to break free of its confines entirely.

"You feel that?" he asks, his voice vibrating in my ears. "That instinct to swallow as the sweetness lingers on the tip of your tongue," He pauses and breathes in passionately through his nose. "But you resist. You keep it in place no matter how tempting." he continues, "Well that's my fucking life, Sienna. Constantly resisting the urge to consume you entirely."

"And yet, regardless of how much it fights against you, against all your instincts," he adds, a hint of a smirk playing on his lips, "letting this sweet fall off that pretty little tongue is something you haven't even considered, right?"

I shake my head, the motion so subtle it's almost imperceptible. I'm unsure if I even moved at all.

"Sweet," he sneers, his tone laced with venom, "you can fight against me until the day you die, but the thought of letting you go, of losing you, has never once crossed my mind. You're stuck with me, whether you like it or not," he smiles, "and we both know you fucking love it."

Marcus watches me closely, his eyes dark with desire and something else I can't quite place. Riskily, I give in to the sweetness on my tongue and swallow, feeling his intense stare like a heated touch against my skin. Now I consider taking another risk, a big one. The thought lingers in my mind for a few moments as I consider my choices.

Fuck it.

"Then do it." I suggest softly but with confidence. "Consume me."

His eyes widen slightly, caught off guard by my boldness. A slow, predatory smile spreads across his lips as he closes the distance between us, his presence overwhelming. A primal hunger flashes in his eyes, and before I can even react, he's upon me. With a swift, almost feral movement, he grabs me and throws me onto the bed, his strength overpowering. I gasp in surprise, the air knocked out of me as I find myself pinned beneath him.

"Remember, you asked for this." he warns.

Before I can protest or even catch my breath, he's tearing at my clothing with a raw urgency, stripping away the barriers between us. His touch is rough, almost bruising, as he exposes my lower half to him. And then, without a word, he descends upon me with a ferocity that steals my breath away. Gripping to the flesh on my thighs and spreading my legs, his mouth finds me hungrily; his movements unyielding and demanding as he does exactly as I asked. He consumes me. Consumes me with an intensity that leaves me trembling in his grasp.

His tongue darts and thrusts, exploring every inch of me with a fervour that leaves me breathless. Each suck and pull sends shockwaves of pleasure coursing through my body, making my back arch involuntarily. The sound of his lips smacking against my skin fills the room, punctuated by the occasional soft growl escaping his lips.

His hands grip my thighs tightly. Very tightly. Pinching me. Holding me in place as he ravages me with unabashed desire. I can feel his beard stubble against my sensitive skin, adding another layer of slightly painful sensation. His name escapes my lips, a plea for him to stop. *Or to continue.* That part, I haven't quite decided. I feel his hot breath against my skin as he pulls away, a sly smile playing on his lips. Without warning, he spits. His eyes bore into mine, a silent challenge in his gaze as he watches for my reaction.

I have no reaction except to lay my head back onto the bed. I can't comprehend anything happening to me right now. I can't comprehend how one man can be so disrespectful and so rough yet so fucking sexy.
Just as I think it's over, he slaps my inner thigh, hard, causing a squeal to leave my lips. His hand leaving a stinging mark on my skin.

He slowly rubs his hand against my swollen clit, hard and demanding. Suddenly he slides two fingers inside, immediately pumping deeply into me. My nails claw into the sheets and an uncontrollable moan leaves my lips.

"Oh, sweet." he smiles, "You're soaked. You like this, don't you?" His words are barely comprehensible in my mind as fingers continue ramming into me. "Who knew my precious angel would enjoy being used like a dirty little slut?" I can only nod, my body trembling with pleasure as he continues to degrade me.

He grips me roughly once more, pinning my legs up by my side, higher than I even thought they could go. His fingers digging into my flesh as he positions himself over me once again. He drives his tongue into me with a force that borders on painful. But it's a good pain. The kind of pain you miss when it leaves.

And then, without warning, he spits on me once again, aiming purposely for my clit; the act rough and demeaning, but causing a surge of desire to flood through me. He licks up the saliva, his tongue flicking against me as I cry out in pleasure. He replaces his tongue with his fingers once more, as he bites down hard on my inner thigh, his teeth leaving a mark instantly.

He moves to the side of me now, towering over my exposed body. Marcus's fingers bury deep inside me, his other hand gripping my hip as he pumps in and out with aggressive, relentless movements. As he continues to dominate me, he grabs my hair, pulling my head back to expose my neck to him.

"That's it, sweet," he growls, his voice filled with desire and malice. "Come for me. Come hard while I finger-fuck you like the dirty little girl you really are." My pussy clenches around his fingers, desperate for more, desperate for him to ruin me completely.

He pushes into me once more. This time, it's slow, hard and out of pattern. His fingers lingering and vibrating deep inside. I cry out for him as I reach my release, my body convulsing as pleasure engulfs me. The room seems to spin as I reach the pinnacle. As I orgasm, feeling the wetness spread between my legs, he's watching me like a hawk. With a satisfied look, he adjusts himself, witnessing me unravel before him.

Finally, he slides his fingers out of me, but before I can catch my breath he grabs my face, squeezing my cheeks, forcing my mouth open. He leans down, his lips brushing against my ear as he shoves his fingers deep down my throat.

"Suck on them. Taste yourself." I struggle against him, but he holds my head in place, his fingers thrusting in and out of my mouth, choking me slightly as he does so. I obey him and begin to suck. "There you go, good girl." His fingers thrust deeper, his thumb rubbing against my cheek. My eyes water from the force he uses to hold my head but, enjoying the praise, I continue to do as he told me, swallowing my own essence.

He stops, pulling his fingers out of my mouth and wiping a tear from the corner of my eye as I sit up; finally taking in a good deep breath.

"Aww," he taunts with a smirk. "How pathetic, sweet." He steps back, his smirk growing as he studies my reaction before continuing to tease me. "If you can't even handle my fingers, how do you expect to take my dick?" I don't respond, but the thought of it makes me throb with need.

He removes his shirt and crouches in front of me.

"Don't worry, sweet. When I decide to fuck you I'll make sure you handle my cock. I'll make sure you take every fucking inch."

As the filth leaves his mouth all I can do is stare in awe. I gulp and nod like an idiot, not even sure if I'm fully listening. Staring into those gorgeous eyes, seeing the sweat glisten on his perfect face, I'm not certain that he's even real. I'm not certain that *I'm* even real.

"That's it," he continues, "Imagine it. Think about me thrusting deep inside you, stretching you beyond your limits."

Oh, don't worry. I'm imagining it.

"I'm gonna take what I fucking want from you, Sienna. I'll make sure of it. I won't stop until those pretty little tears are streaming down your face."

I believe him, and though I'd never admit it, I can't fucking wait. He stands again, his 6ft4 shirtless body towering over me. The room falls to silence, and he doesn't take his eyes off me, not once, despite the fact that I'm not looking back. I'm looking at his body. It's no secret that Marcus is sexy. I've always known that. But right now, in this moment, it's like I'm seeing him for the first time all over again.

My eyes trace the lines of his chest, where beads of sweat cling to the taut muscles, highlighting every ripple and ridge. His abs are a work of art, sculpted and defined. As his chest rises and falls, his dark hair lies tousled and damp from the effort he just exerted into pleasing me.

He chuckles lightly as he watches me ogling him, the dimple on his cheek sitting deep.

"What you thinking about?"

"I don't think I've ever noticed that tattoo," I blurt out. He's covered in them, and I pay attention to them; or so I thought, "Is it new?" I ask, finally looking back up at him.

"I did it myself a few nights ago." he replies calmly.

"It's a spider."

"Correct," he laughs. "A shy one."

Marcus winks at me, his smile intimate and genuine. I try to hide my grin by biting my lip, but it's no use. I'm too flattered. He really is obsessed with me. The mere consideration of having my character from his book permanently inked onto his skin is so incredibly beautiful.

"I like it." I whisper.

"Sorry, you *like* one of my tattoos?"

"Just that one."

"Well, I guess I'll have to consider keeping that one then."

"Funny," I say, my eyes roaming his body once again. "You genuinely don't have room for any more. Well, unless you plan on getting one down there." I add with a mischievous grin, gesturing subtly to the bulge in his grey tracksuit bottoms.

"I think 'Choking Hazard' would be quite fitting."

"Gross."

My eyes linger on Marcus's chest, tracing the lines of his muscles as he chuckles, the sound like music to my ears. His dimple deepens, a crease of pleasure etching itself on his face, and I'm caught in the undertow of his charm, my heart swelling with a warmth that's hard to ignore. He leans in, pressing a gentle kiss to my forehead, his lips warm against my skin.

"You're fucking adorable, sweet." he murmurs, his voice low and affectionate. I smile up at him, my heart fluttering in my chest at his words.

I watch as Marcus reaches for a joint, deft fingers rolling it with practised ease. As he lights it, the room is filled with the earthy scent of cannabis. Taking a puff, he exhales slowly, the smoke curling around him like a wisp of temptation. His eyes meet mine, a glimmer of mischief dancing within them as he speaks.

"Now, naughty girl." he mumbles, the joint held between his teeth "Get some sleep," he says, his voice low and teasing, a hint of authority underlying his words.

"Okay."

CHAPTER 11:
TRACKER TROUBLE

Dean

Skylar walks out of her room and, as usual, she immediately begins to verbally assault me.

"What the fuck are you doing?"

I shimmy myself out from underneath the car to respond, as this pink-haired dictator looks down at me; a very scary iced coffee in her hand.

"Ice skating." I respond sarcastically.

"Dickhead." she scowls. "For real though, what are you doing?"

"Thank you so much for that completely unnecessary insult." she doesn't respond and instead just scrunches her nose up at me, "I'm making sure there isn't a tracker." Skylar's eyebrows shoot up in surprise, followed by a burst of laughter.

"A tracker? Who do you think you are, James Bond?" she mocks, taking a sip of her iced coffee, causing me to wonder where the fuck she got an iced coffee from and why she didn't get one for me. I sigh and continue inspecting the underside of the car.

"I took it from Razor's warehouse." I explain.

"So? They're not the Mafia."

My God, she gets more insufferable by the minute.

"That's not the point. He works for Grizzly, that's nothing to scoff at."

"Paranoid much? Maybe it's the shitty weed you smoke."

"Could you do me a favour, Sky?" I ask in an attempt to set her up; intending to follow with a 'fuck off'.

"No." she replies bluntly, completely slaughtering my joke. I slide out from under the car with a dramatic huff, standing up and brushing off imaginary dirt like a failed car mechanic wannabe.

"Look, I don't have time for your babbling."

"You know, if these guys do catch you, can I have your gun collection?"

"Sure, I'll put it in my will."

I get back to business, poking and prodding around the engine components. There's no way Grizzly's men haven't slapped trackers on their vehicles; and I'm not about to be caught off guard. As I delve deeper into the engine bay, my fingers graze something metallic. With a careless flick of my wrist, I reach for what seems like an innocent wire, only to be met with a surge of electricity that shoots all the way up my arm.

"Fuck!" I shout, as my body is thrown backwards.

The pain is unbearable, like a thousand needles stabbing me all at once. My muscles seize up, and I swear I'm staring down the Grim Reaper himself. Sparks fly, and for a moment, all I can see is blinding white light. The smell of burnt flesh fills the air, and my heart feels like it's about to leap out of my chest. Skylar, startled by my very embarrassing electrocution, rushes over, her eyes wide with panic.

"Dean! Oh my God, are you okay?" I can barely form words, still reeling from the shock, instead I nod, catching my breath.

Skylar's face pales as she looks down at my hand and realises the severity of the situation. My skin instantly blistered and my hand trembling beyond description.

"Shit, we need to get you to a hospital."

"No," I insist snappily, "I'm fine, honestly. Just give me a minute."

I sit there, shock still coursing through me. I begin to think and dwell on the series of near misses I've encountered recently. The incident in the car, the tree falling out of nowhere, now this? It's like I'm constantly dancing on the edge of a blade, tempting fate with every step.

Skylar's concerned voice cuts through my thoughts, pulling me back to the present.

"Dean? You okay?" I blink, realising I've been lost in my own head for God knows how long.

"Yeah, I'm fine," I mutter as I pull myself up onto my feet, trying to push aside the mounting nerves gnawing at my insides. But deep down, I know I'm not fooling anyone; least of all Skylar.

She raises an eyebrow, clearly not buying my feeble reassurance.

"You sure? You look a little fucked up." I hesitate, unsure how to put my sudden existential crisis into words. But as I look into Skylar's eyes, so full of genuine concern, I know I shouldn't keep it bottled.

"It's just, this is the third time after leaving London that I've almost been killed. I nearly crashed the car on the way down here; and when that tree fell down," I explain pointing at the tree next to my room, "it was as if it was aiming right at me." Sky listens intently, as she quickly pans her eyes to the fallen tree. "I don't know, Sky. I'm sure I'm overthinking, but after this it feels like I may be tempting fate."

Skylar bites her nail and scrunches her face, which suggests to me that something is concerning her.

"What?" I ask softly.

"I probably shouldn't bring it up, but do you think it could be related to the book in some way?" I shake my head adamantly, the idea of the book having anything to do with anything else in our lives isn't something I even want to entertain.

"Nah." I reply, dismissing the notion outright, "We sealed it tight. The book is dead and buried."

Skylar nods, a smile gracing her face. But it's weak, and it doesn't quite reach her eyes.

"Yeah, you're right." she says, though her voice lacks conviction. "It's probably just your karma for dealing dodgy drugs." I muster the energy to grin at Skylar's quip, enjoying the banter.

I feign a cough, my hands settling lightly on my knees as I pretend to double over, a ruse designed to unnerve Skylar. Her eyes dart towards me, and she startles, her hand shooting out to settle on my back in a gesture of concern.

"You good?" she asks.

"Yeah fine," I say, purposefully straining my voice "Can you just do me a favour?"

"Yeah, of course-" Skylar begins, but I cut her off abruptly with a forceful push, shoving her onto the grass beside us.

"Fuck off." I retort, the words laced with playful aggression.

"Dean!"

CHAPTER 12:

BREAKING THE RULE

Sienna

ONE WEEK LATER.

It's 6:24p.m.

Marcus left the room to go and talk to Dean about an hour ago.

He forgot to lock the door.

I've spent the last hour thinking. My mind keeps circling back through the same mismatched thoughts, like a record stuck on repeat. I don't particularly care about escaping this place. Sure, I miss my mother, but the truth is I would miss Marcus a whole lot more. I want to be here with him. Yet, there's an undeniable urge within me to get out, to see the countryside, to know where I am exactly, to just breathe some fresh air.

Be a little rebellious.
Prove a point.

My brain is entirely split, torn between conflicting desires. So many thoughts running through me that my mind is eerily silent. I need a break from this room. But Marcus made it clear that if I left, he would punish me.

And the unsettling part is, I think I want him to punish me.

But it's not right, is it? Marcus keeping me here like this. I should be screaming for freedom, for the autonomy to make my own choices. But what if I enjoy being treated like this? Is that so wrong? That I enjoy the way he controls me, protects me.

I've been trying to figure out why he hasn't gone the full way with me, despite me finally admitting that I wanted it. It's a persistent itch I can't scratch.

But I'm sure this would push him there.

The question is can I handle it? Is he bluffing, using fear to keep me tethered to his side? To keep me safe. Or does he truly intend to push me to my limits? Break me entirely. I'm battling with my morality but deep down I know exactly what I want. All I want right now is to be at his mercy, to feel the weight of his control bearing down on me. I want to be degraded, humiliated, ruined beyond recognition. It's a twisted desire, one that I can hardly bring myself to admit, even to myself.

But it's the truth.

With it settled in my mind, I bite the bullet. I head towards the door and make my way outside. The warm evening air kisses my skin as I take a deep dramatic breath. A soft glow over the landscape illuminates my path as I cautiously sneak my way past the cottage where Marcus is undoubtedly preoccupied.

Every rustle of the bushes and crunch of gravel beneath my feet feels amplified in the stillness of the evening, heightening my awareness of the risk I'm taking. The urge to glance back, to ensure I haven't been detected, tugs at the corners of my mind, but I resist. The countryside stretches out before me, vast and inviting, with fields of verdant green rolling gently into the horizon.

I wander aimlessly, revelling in the sensation of grass beneath my feet and the whisper of the wind in my ears. Every step feels like a tiny victory for me. Like I'm getting back that teasing sliver of control I used to have over him. I drink in the beauty of the landscape, letting the sights and sounds fill me. It's peaceful. So peaceful, and I wish Marcus was here to see it with me.

As I perch against a weathered fence, watching the sun sink below the horizon, a sense of tranquillity washes over me. The sky transforms into a canvas of fiery hues, casting a warm, aureate glow over the landscape. The distant chirping of crickets and the gentle rustle of leaves in the breeze form a comforting backdrop, lulling me into a momentary state of peace and reverie.

For a while, I allow myself to simply exist in this serene setting, letting the beauty of the evening envelop me. The colours of the sky deepen, painting streaks of orange and pink across the heavens, and I find myself mesmerised by the dance of light and shadow.

But amidst the breathtaking beauty of the sunset, memories of my parents begin to seep into my thoughts like gentle whispers. I close my eyes, allowing their faces to materialise in my mind's eye. I miss them so much. The pain of their absence is like a wound that never fully heals, a constant ache that's always there, lingering beneath the surface. They were good people. Pure. Quiet. Tears prick at the corners of my eyes as I remember them; my father's warm smile, my mother's gentle touch. I recall the small, everyday moments we shared. But the memories are tainted by the pain of their loss, their sudden and brutal deaths.

I'll never forget the day they were taken from me. The visions I have about their final moments. It must have been terrifying for them.

I recall the way my father's eyes would light up when he spoke of the kind of love I deserve; the kind that would cradle, cherish and shield me, that would accept me without condition. He'd whisper stories of the person who would one day make my heart sing, who would love me with an unwavering devotion.

Marcus is that person.

Sure, he's not a perfect person. Far from it. In fact, he's a very bad person, evil even. But he's good to me. There's a fierceness in him; a pure and obsessive determination to love me and keep me safe at all costs, that I know my father would appreciate. He looks at me the same way my dad used to look at my mum. As if she was the centre of his entire universe.

With a heavy heart, I watch as the last traces of daylight fade into darkness. Each flicker of light extinguished feels like a small farewell.

Hours slip by unnoticed as I sit there, under the stars, alone with my thoughts. And then, as if from out of the darkness itself, I'm startled by the sound of gravel crunching. A car approaches. A black car with tinted windows, its engine purring softly as it slows almost to a stop behind me. Its presence is ominous and creepy. Cold, paralysing fear grips my heart. The hairs on the back of my neck stand on end as a shiver runs down my spine.

Instinctively, I rise to my feet, my heart pounding in my chest as I watch the car slowly pass me. On autopilot, I rise to my feet, my eyes fixed on the receding brake lights. I think it's time to leave.

As I approach the cottage, my paranoia begins to seep into my bones like a chill. Every flicker of movement, every creak of a branch, seems to take on a menacing quality. I'm convinced that the shadows themselves are closing in on me. But as I pause, my breath fogging in the misty air, I begin to realise I'm probably being overly dramatic. My imagination is running riot, conjuring up monsters from every tree and rock. Maybe Marcus was right. I shouldn't have wandered out here on my own.

I walk back past Dean's cottage and notice the lights off. Marcus must have gone back. Standing at the door, I feel a wild mix of nerves and, dare I say it, excitement. I know he'll be furious that I left and I don't know what insane punishment he's planning on giving me, yet here I stand, holding in my squeals of excitement over the thought of it. I hover there, hand trembling over the door handle, battling with myself. Should I go in? Or should I wait, relish in this moment of defiance a little longer?

But as the door swings open and I'm yanked into the room by my hair, it's safe to say the decision is made on my behalf.

CHAPTER 13:
CONSEQUENCES

Marcus

As I sit on the edge of the bed, I'm well aware that one of two things have happened here. Either Sienna is genuinely attempting to get away from me and therefore I'm about to spend my night riding around until I find her; or she's about to walk back in here and realise just how serious my threats are.

Though she'd never give me the credit, I know Sienna now. I know exactly how she works. Exactly what she's thinking. She wouldn't leave. She's testing me. She wants me to crack. She's desperate for it. I see the hunger in her eyes. She wants more, and maybe I should've already given it to her. I was trying not to push her too far, but clearly I didn't push her far enough; and that's about to change.

Then it happens. I hear Sienna's footsteps approaching on the gravel outside. I rise from the bed with a controlled grace and crack my neck. I approach the door, shifting all my weight with each slow, calculated step. A predator stalking its prey, my senses sharp and attuned to every sound and movement.

As the door handle twitches under her hesitant touch, a smirk twists my lips into a smug grin. The poor thing. So fucking cute. She's second-guessing herself, debating whether she should face the storm she's unleashed. The thought elicits another low laugh, a primal sound that reverberates with a promise of impending retribution.

In one swift motion, I yank open the door, the wood slamming against the wall with a satisfying thud. Before Sienna can react, I grab a fistful of her hair, and pull her into the room with a forceful tug, shutting the door instantly behind us. She stumbles forward, caught off guard by my sudden aggression, but I show no mercy. With one hand tangled in her hair, I pull her close, feeling the heat radiating off her skin. My other hand finds her wrists, twisting them behind her back, pinning her against me.

"Look who decided to come back."

"I can explain-" I give her no time to even think of an explanation before I snatch her, lifting her off her feet and carrying her towards the dining table. The moment we reach it, I slam her down onto the wooden surface, her back meeting the cold, hard material with a thud. Her eyes widen further as she struggles to catch her breath, her body arching slightly under the sudden impact.

Quickly, I position myself above her, pinning her arms above her head with one hand, my other hand resting on the table next to her face.

"If I knew you were this desperate to take my fucking cock, I would've given it to you sooner." I say before I rip off her shorts and throw them to the ground.

Pulling out my butterfly knife from my pocket, I watch her pupils dilate.

"I don't want-" she lies.

"Then why did you come back? Huh?"

I grip the handle of the knife, my fingers tightening around it, feeling the cold steel beneath my touch. With a stern face, I slide the knife's blade under the fabric of her top, cutting through it with a rough, unyielding motion. The material parts like a curtain, revealing her bare skin.

Her eyes, filled with a mixture of fear and desire, meet mine as I continue to cut, the knife dancing over her skin, leaving a trail of goosebumps in its wake. The knife glides through her knickers next, tearing the fabric away from her body, leaving her exposed and vulnerable.

"Marcus, please-"

"Then fight, sweet. Show me what you've got." I growl, my voice dripping with menace as I press the tip of the knife against her skin, tracing lazy circles along her beautiful body.

She hesitates for a moment, her body tense with anticipation. And then, with a sudden burst of strength, she obeys. She kicks out at me, her movements frantic but not entirely serious. There's no conviction. It's a feeble attempt to fight me off. She wants this and I'm more than happy to oblige.

But hey, at least she's learning to follow orders.

As much as I'd love to kiss that gorgeous fucking body and hold her close, I don't waste time on pleasantries or pretences. This is punishment, and I intend to make it crystal clear. I spit on her pretty little pussy, the saliva landing with a small splatter on her sensitive skin. A weak attempt to lubricate her. Then, without any hesitation, I thrust my fingers into her, not caring if it hurts. Hoping it hurts.

As I finger fuck her roughly, I can feel her muscles clenching around my fingers, her body trying to find some semblance of pleasure amidst the pain. Her body continues to tremble and she tries to catch her breath, but the sensation from my fingers still inside her persists.

"Marcus, stop." she whines pathetically. I smirk, enjoying the sight of her vulnerability.

"Stop? I'm just getting started, sweet." I reply, my fingers still thrusting inside her, my grip on her wrists tightening. I'm not stopping. She doesn't want that. I'm going to make her come, over and over again. I want her arousal dripping down my fingers.

I increase the pace, enjoying the sight of her struggling against my invasion. I twist my fingers, exploring her depths, making sure she knows I'm in control. Her body responds to my touch, her hips bucking against my hand, but I hold her in place, her legs spread wide, her body at my mercy.

The minutes pass, and her moans become more frenzied, her body trembling with anticipation. I can feel her tight walls clenching around my fingers, and I know she's close.

Then, without warning, she cries out in pleasure as she comes against her will. Her body convulses, her eyes wide with a mix of shock, pain, and the raw intensity of her unwanted orgasm.

"Did I tell you to fucking come? Huh?" I ask. As she shakes her head, I deliver a sharp slap to her swollen clit, causing her to squeal in pain. I force her legs apart even wider, spreading her come-soaked pussy with my fingers, making sure they're covered.

As I stand over her trembling body, I hold my fingers up.

"Look at the mess you've made." I say, my voice dripping with disdain. I slowly spread her come across my fingers, making sure she can see. I watch her eyes widen, a mix of shame and arousal still present.

I know she's caught between wanting more and hating me for it. But that's exactly what her punishment is.

I slowly bring my fingers to my mouth, savouring the taste of her. No drop going to waste. The act intended to degrade her further, to show her that, at this moment, she's nothing more than a fucktoy for my pleasure. And it's all her fault.

I drag her from the table and position her over my knee as I sit on the edge of the bed. I hold her securely, her hands bound behind her back as I trace my fingers slowly down her body, each touch a teasing promise of the pain to come.

"Why did you leave, Sienna?" I ask calmly.

"I'm sorry." I spank her ass hard, my hand connecting with her flesh in a rough, deliberate motion.

"That's not an answer."

"I-I don't know." In response, I deliver another swat to her ass, this time harder and more forceful. My hand leaving a burning sensation that she can't ignore.

"Don't lie to me." I pull firmer on her restrained wrists and a whimper leaves her lips. "You wanted me to fucking punish you. Right?" I taunt, my voice dripping with malice before I strike her again. She manages a faint "Yes," her voice shaking with emotion.

I dig my nails into her skin and scratch up the back of her thigh, followed by one more smack to her ass, causing her to cry out even louder; her body trembling under the force of my hand. As a tear rolls down her cheek, I taunt her.

"It's okay to cry, little one. I enjoy seeing you weep for me." I wet two fingers with spit and push them back inside her cunt. Pumping slowly.

"*This* time, sweet, you have my permission. I'll give you thirty seconds, and you better fucking come." I have no intention of timing her. My angel can take as long as she wants, but I don't want her knowing that. Her moans fill the otherwise-silent room as I twist and drive my fingers deep inside her. My rhythm is steady.

"Time is ticking, pretty." I taunt. I feel her inner walls clenching around my fingers, a desperate grip of submission pulling me deeper into her abyss. Each quake that racks her body sending vibrations of primal satisfaction coursing through me. Her ass bouncing with every jolt of my fingers. I press closer, my breath a searing brand against her ear

"Are you learning your lesson?" She doesn't respond, I don't expect her to. And then, with a final, guttural wail, she capitulates utterly, her body a vessel for the overwhelming sensations crashing over her.

She collapses against me, spent and trembling; the dripping evidence of her obedience covering my fingers. I don't stop. With a predatory grin, I continue to ravish her relentlessly. I increase the pressure of my fingers, pushing her past the point of pleasure into a realm of pure agony. She's already broken. She's mine, completely and utterly, to use and abuse as I please. And I'll make sure she never forgets it.

I stare down at her, bruised and crying, and whisper close to her body.

"You think you can take more, sweet?" Reluctantly, and to my genuine surprise, she nods her head, a silent agreement to endure more of my cruelty.

"Are you sure?" I confirm, raising an eyebrow.

"Yes, I'm sure."

She can't be real.

"Good, because I'm not done with you yet."

With a sadistic grin, I drag her back to the dining table, her body limp and battered from the intense session we've just endured. I bend her over the table, her arms still pinned behind her back, her body now completely at my mercy. As I position myself behind her, I grip the butterfly knife once again. The cold steel glints in the dim light, a stark contrast to the warmth of her skin. I press the blade against the side of her neck.

"You know, sweet, I was planning on being gentle when I took your virginity," I whisper into her ear, my voice dripping with malice, "but clearly, that's not what you want." I pull my dick out of my joggers, "You want pain? You're gonna fucking get it."

I stab the knife down into the table next to her, causing her to flinch, before I position myself at her entrance, the head of my cock pressing against her sensitive skin. I can feel her muscles tense, her body trying to resist. With a forceful thrust, I enter her, burying myself deep inside her in one swift motion, her pussy tearing as I stretch her. She cries out. I hold her hips, my grip firm, as I begin to move within her, my thrusts slow and deliberate at first, but quickly building.

Her body responds to my every move, her moans filling the room as I claim her, her tight walls gripping me in a way that leaves me both breathless and enraged.

"Ass up, Sienna. Show me what belongs to me." I order. Her body trembles as she obeys, her ass arching up to accommodate my savage thrusts as I completely ravage her; my cock plunging into her depths.

"That's it, sweet. Take every fucking inch. My dirty little slut." I slam into her, my body moving with a ferocity that leaves her breathless.

Her cries grow louder, her body arching to meet mine, her submission evident in every movement. As I notice a tiny drop of blood I'm like a fucking shark. The sight of her torn cunt being assaulted by my cock only fueling my aggression further.

"You're doing so well, beautiful. Such a brave girl." I grip her throat, my fingers digging into her delicate skin. She tries to struggle, but I hold her in place, my eyes locked onto her.

"Remember, you deserve this. I warned you. I'm gonna have my fucking way with you until *I* decide you've had enough."

I can feel my release drawing near and the thought of filling her with my come isn't even a debate. I smack her ass and grab her hair again, using it to control her movements.

"Are you ready to take my come, sweet?"
She doesn't reply. I pull out slightly, my cock glistening with her arousal, I look down at her and issue my command.

"Beg for my come. Beg me to fill that tight little pussy." She doesn't. Instead she continues to whimper and cry. Not good enough. Seeing her faux-reluctance, I decide to force it out of her. I press the tip of my thumb against her asshole, causing her to flinch and cry out in pain. Her body tenses, but I don't relent.

"Now, Sienna. Beg."

"Fuck-" she mumbles, "Please." I press harder.

"Please what?"

"Please.. fill me." Hearing her beg, I remove my thumb.

"Good girl, there you go. I'll make sure I give you every last fucking drop." With that, I push my cock back into her, feeling her pussy clench around me in response. I pull her hair even tighter, forcing her to arch her back and take my dick deeper than ever before. "Fuck, Sienna. You feel so good."

As I reach my release, I continue to fuck her with reckless abandon, my dick sliding in and out of her wet pussy with a lewd slapping sound. With a final, powerful thrust, I release my come into her, as deep as possible, filling her with the evidence of her degradation. I can feel the warm liquid spilling inside her, coating her walls. I stay buried inside her for a few moments, making sure she takes all of me. I pull out slowly, my cock glistening with fluid, feeling her pussy grip me.

As I step back, I spit on her one last time, a final act of degradation before I leave her there, lying in the aftermath of our encounter. My come leaking from her hole. Her panting, spent body trembling. I've claimed her now. Taken her in the most brutal way possible.

"God, look at you. You're so fucking beautiful."

I pull up my joggers and approach her slowly, my steps deliberate and purposeful, until I'm standing right beside her, looking down at her trembling form. With a predatory gleam in my eyes, I crouch down to her eye level, my glare piercing through her.

"Sweet," I growl, my voice low and commanding. "Don't you ever leave this fucking room again." I reach out and grab her chin, forcing her to look at me. Tears still filling her eyes. "Do you understand?" She nods weakly. She knows better than to disobey me now.

CHAPTER 14:
BUTTER
Marcus

I wake up my sleeping angel with a rough shake, my hand gripping her delicate shoulder.

"Wake up, sweet," I growl, my voice low and commanding. She stirs, blinking sleepily as she tries to focus on me.

"What's.. what's going on?" she mumbles, her voice groggy. I can't help but admire the way her hair tumbles across her pillow, her tousled curls framing her face in a way that makes my heart skip a beat. But I push those thoughts aside, focusing on the matter at hand. Ignoring her question, I press on.

"What sandwiches do you like the most?" I demand, my tone brooking no argument. She blinks, taken aback by the abruptness of my random question.

"Um, I don't know," she stammers, her confusion evident. I grit my teeth, playful frustration simmering beneath the surface.

"Well, figure it out," I snap, "I'm not asking again." With a sigh, she nods, understanding the urgency in my tone.

"Okay, okay," she says, scrambling to gather her thoughts. She bites her bottom lip briefly and a tiny 'hm' comes from her mouth.

She's perfect. She really is fucking perfect.
I can't take my eyes off her.

Finally, she speaks, her voice hesitant.

"Ham and cheese?" she says, her words tentative. I nod, a small smile tugging at the corners of my lips.

"Good choice," I say, my tone softer now. "Now hurry up and get ready. We're going out."

A little while later, Sienna finally saunters out of the bedroom. My eyes roam over her, taking in every inch of her beauty, and for a moment, I forget how to fucking breathe. She's wearing a short white dress with a corset top that accentuates her curves and a puffy out skirt that sways with each step she takes. My eyes practically devour her as she approaches.

"Jesus Christ." I say, licking my lips; my hand rising to cover my smirk. Sienna grins at my words, a playful glint dancing in her eyes. She knows she's got me twisted around her little finger, and she's loving every second.

Without another word, I hold the door open for her, nodding my head for her to walk out. She struts slowly past me, her eyes deliberately never leaving mine, like she's daring me to make a move.

Little fucking tease.

Her perfume punches me and my jaw clenches as I fight the urge to grab and fuck her right then and there.

I lead her outside to where my bike waits, its sleek black frame gleaming in the morning light. I step closer to Sienna, my fingers lingering as I lift the helmet from where it rests. With a deliberate slowness, I lower it over her head, the straps cinching tight as our eyes meet.

"There you go, sweet. Can't have you getting hurt now can we?" I say with a wink, alluding to last night's events. I bring her hand to my lips, pressing a tender kiss to her skin before helping her onto the bike. As Sienna adjusts herself on the seat, I slide my hand across her waist, resting it there for longer than necessary. My thumb gliding back and forth.

I ride her out for around half an hour, speeding the entirety of the way, until I park up at a field. The engine's roar fading away as I kill it. The field is reminiscent of the one I had taken her to before. Except this one is covered in a dreamy array of flowers. I lift off Sienna's helmet with a flourish, revealing her blooming hair and those honey brown eyes. The sunlight painting golden hues across her; a vision of ethereal beauty.

I hold out my hand for her to grab onto and instead she grabs onto just my outer two fingers, and I can't help but chuckle. It might be the cutest fucking thing I've ever seen.

Together, we stroll through the field, the flowers swaying in the gentle zephyr like they're putting on a show just for us. I lead her to a shadier spot beneath the sprawling branches of a large tree, where the sunlight filters through the leaves in dappled patterns. With a quick search in my bag, I retrieve the blanket and sandwiches I had tucked away earlier.

"Isn't this...?" she starts, trailing off as realisation dawns on her face. I give a low chuckle,

"Yes, it's the blanket from your bed," I reply, my tone casual. "I hope you don't mind that I borrowed it for our little date."

Sienna smiles and scrunches her nose.

"A date, huh?" she asks, amusement evident in her voice. I nod, not bothering to elaborate.

"Of course."

We settle on the blanket, the air heavy with the scent of flowers and the warmth of the sun. I nod towards the sandwiches.

"Eat." I say, my tone gruff but not unkind. She takes a bite.

"Mm, very nice." she says, a genuine smile on her lips.

"What can I say? I pride myself on my culinary skills." I joke, knowing full well all I did was slap some ham and cheese between two slices of bread. She laughs, her eyes sparkling.

"You're quite the chef," she teases, her tone playful. I raise an eyebrow, a grin spreading across my face.

"Oh, you haven't seen anything yet, sweet." I reply, leaning in closer. "I make a mean bacon sandwich that you'll have to try." Her laughter fills the air, the sound like music to my ears. She bites her bottom lip and looks down briefly before her eye contact intensifies; those beautiful eyes twinkling with mischief.

"There's something else of yours I'd like to taste."

What the fuck.

My heart skips a beat, her boldness catching me completely off guard. I swallow hard and clear my throat, my mind racing as I try to regain my composure.

"Excuse me?" I ask. But Sienna's expression instantly morphs back into one of oblivious curiosity as she meets my gaze. Then, with a playful glint in her eyes, she simply says,

"Nothing," her tone innocent but loaded with suggestive undertones.

I shift discreetly, trying to hide the growing bulge in my pants. Did that really just happen?

Fucking hell, Sienna.

I guess this is what I get when I try to be romantic. Her eyes flicker down for a moment, and then a proud smile tugs at the corner of her lips. Oh God, she's noticed. But instead of commenting or making a fuss, she just gives me this sly look, like she's silently congratulating herself on getting under my skin. Lucky for me, Sienna's attention is suddenly diverted by something in front of us.

"Ooh, look!" she exclaims, her voice bubbling with excitement.

I follow her eye-line to see a butterfly fluttering nearby, its delicate yellow wings catching the sunlight.

Relief floods through me, grateful for the timely distraction.

"Yeah, wow. Look at that." I reply, doing my best to sound enthusiastic.

I watch in awe as Sienna's eyes light up with childlike wonder as she follows the delicate movements of the butterfly. She reaches out a hand, her fingers trembling with anticipation, as if she's afraid the slightest movement might scare it away.

"Isn't it just the most beautiful thing?" she asks. I nod, my gaze fixed not on the butterfly, but on her.

"Yeah, it really is," I reply, my voice barely audible over the soft rustle of the leaves.

As Sienna reaches out to touch the butterfly, a gentle breeze sweeps through the field, causing her hair to dance around her face like golden threads in the sunlight. The butterfly lands gracefully on her outstretched hand, its delicate wings quivering against her skin. She gasps softly, her eyes widening in amazement as she holds her breath, afraid to disturb the fragile creature. And in this instant, she's the most enchanting sight I've ever beheld. She's like a dream made flesh.

Sienna's fingers trace the delicate, iridescent patterns on the butterfly's wings, her touch gentle and reverent. The butterfly seems to respond to her, its movements growing even more graceful as if in acknowledgment of her tender care. After a moment, she reluctantly tries to release the butterfly, her hand opening slowly as she lets it go. But instead of flying away, the butterfly hovers nearby, as if reluctant to leave her side. Sienna's ebullient laughter fills the air.

"It wants to stay." she exclaims, her eyes sparkling with excitement.

"Looks like you've made a new friend, sweet." I tease, unable to hide my awe at the magical moment.

Sienna's smile still lingers on her face as she settles back onto the blanket beside me, the butterfly's delicate wings still dancing against her hand. She scoots closer, her radiant warmth seeping into my side as she leans into me, her soft breath a gentle caress against my skin.

Just as we melt into the peaceful moment, a large black car rumbles by on the road where we parked the bike. Sienna's expression tightens, her eyebrows scrunching together as she watches the car pass by.

"What's wrong?" I ask. Sienna hesitates before answering, her eyes still fixed on the retreating car.

"Nothing," she says, but I can tell by the tension in her voice that she's hiding something.

"Sure?"

"Yes, I'm sure."

She shakes her head and proceeds to hold out her hand towards me, her eyes alight with anticipation.

"Your turn, tough guy," she says, her voice filled with excitement. I grin as I hold out my hand for the butterfly to walk onto. To my surprise, the tiny creature flutters over and lands gently on my outstretched palm, its delicate legs tickling my skin. Sienna's smile widens as she watches. "See, it likes you too," she says, her voice filled with affection.

I raise an eyebrow.

"You should give it a name." I suggest, passing back our new little buddy. Sienna doesn't miss a beat.

"Butter," she declares, a pure smile playing on her lips. I can't help but chuckle at the simplicity of her choice.

"Butter it is." I reply, feeling a strange sense of fondness for the little creature.

After spending some time basking in the tranquillity of the field, Sienna and I reluctantly rise to our feet, ready to make our way back to the bike. But as we start to gather our things, Sienna hesitates, her eyes fixed on Butter, who is now sitting leisurely on her shoulder.

"I don't want to leave Butter here." she says, her voice filled with concern as she pouts her bottom lip. I glance down at the butterfly, understanding her reluctance.

"We can't exactly take it with us, sweet." I reply, feeling a pang of guilt at the thought of leaving her beloved Butter behind.

She doesn't reply, instead just stares up at me with the saddest, most guilt-tripping eyes I've ever seen.

I sigh, knowing there's no arguing with her when she gets like this. I rummage through my bag, coming up with her small Tupperware container I had brought for the sandwiches. Without a word, I reach for my butterfly knife, flipping it open with practised ease. Sienna's eyes widen in surprise as I press the tip of the blade against the lid of the container.

"What are you doing?" she asks. But I simply shake my head, a small smile playing on my lips.

"Trust me," I reply, as I stab several holes in the lid of the Tupperware. Sienna watches in silence, her eyes fixed on my hands as I work. And as I finish, I hold up the container for her to see, a satisfied grin on my face.

"There," I say, "now Butter can breathe."

Sienna's face breaks into a relieved smile as she gazes at the container in her hands. She delicately places Butter into the container and shuts the lid before looking back up to me.

"Thank you."

"You're welcome." I reply, kissing her forehead before grabbing her bike helmet. As I hand it to her, she looks up at me with a teasing glint in her eyes.

"You really need to stop stabbing things though." I breathe out a soft laugh.

"I'll think about it." I reply with a playful wink.

CHAPTER 15:
THE BARN

Dean

"You know, when you mentioned 'exploring'," Skylar starts in her usual sarcastic tone, "I assumed maybe a nice stroll in the woods, find some animals, maybe a little cafe somewhere. But no, apparently Dean Douglas' idea of 'exploring' means walking at 50 miles an hour down dead-end country lanes!" My patience wears thin as I glance at Skylar.

"Genuinely, do you ever shut the fuck up?" I hear Skylar's laboured breaths as she struggles to keep up, her words coming out in gasps.

"I will if you slow the fuck down!"

"That's a lie."

"You know, Sky, maybe if you focused on actually leaving your bedroom once in a while instead of yapping, you wouldn't be struggling to keep up." Skylar's glare intensifies, but she doesn't miss a beat.

"If you weren't such an impatient asshole I wouldn't *need* to keep up." I let out a bark of laughter, unable to resist the opportunity to annoy her further.

"It's hard to have patience when you're forced to babysit her royal highness all the fucking time."

"I swear, if I collapse from exhaustion it's on you."

"Oh, and what a tragedy that would be." I reply, my voice laced with faux concern.

"You're a cunt."

"Guilty as charged."

We keep walking, and Skylar just won't quit her griping. I figured a bit of wandering would be a nice distraction while Marcus and Sienna are off fucking or whatever it is they do; but it seems Skylar can't muster up a positive thought to save her life.
But then, out of the corner of my eye, I spot a big, old, empty-looking barn looming in the distance, its weathered wood and rusty roof standing out against the landscape like a sore thumb. I grunt in acknowledgment, feeling a flicker of curiosity despite Skylar's sour mood.

"That's pretty cool." I remark, nodding towards the barn, my tone tinged with genuine interest.

"Dean, it's a fucking barn."

"Wow, you're a genius."

Drawing nearer, I'm struck by the sheer size of the barn. It looms over us like a behemoth, its weathered facade whispering tales of years gone by. It's not just big, it's massive; a towering monument to the past.

"Holy shit," I mutter under my breath, taking in the barn's impressive stature. "This thing's huge." Skylar, still lagging behind, lets out an evil giggle.

"Bet you've never heard that before."

Ignoring her jibe, I push open the barn door and step inside, the musty scent of hay and dust hitting me like a wave. As we step into the barn, our eyes immediately fixate on the towering presence of a massive combine harvester. Its sheer size and mechanical complexity stand out amidst the dusty interior, a testament to a bygone era of farming.

"Sick," I breathe, my voice hushed with awe as I take in the sight of the imposing machine. To my surprise, Skylar's usual attitude gives way to genuine interest as she steps closer to the combine harvester, her eyes scanning its intricate details with fascination.

"That *is* pretty cool." I nod in agreement, a smile tugging at the corners of my lips as I watch Skylar's unexpected enthusiasm.

While Skylar climbs up into the driver's seat of the combine harvester, eager to explore its inner workings, I continue to wander through the barn, my curiosity leading me to other relics scattered throughout the space. I find myself drawn to a collection of old farming tools lining the walls; rusted ploughs, weathered pitchforks, and battered scythes.

I'm definitely taking some of this shit.

"Dean, check this out!" she calls, her voice echoing through the barn. As I make my way over to the combine harvester, Skylar's fingers dance across the control panel, her grin widening with each button she presses. With a mischievous grin, Skylar points to the control panel. "Watch this," she says, her fingers dancing across the switches and buttons. With a flick of her wrist, she activates the lights, illuminating the interior of the barn with a powerful glow. "Pretty cool, huh?" she says, her eyes shining with pride. I nod, impressed by her discovery.

"Yeah, not bad."

As I run my fingers over the sea of blades I can't help but feel a sense of wonder at the machinery before me. It's not every day you get to explore something like this. It's the same rush I get doing graffiti and working on cars; tinkering with engines and machinery. There's something about the raw power and precision that gets my adrenaline pumping. I can't help but be drawn in, my mind racing as I try to figure out how the whole thing works.

Lost in my own exploration, I barely register Skylar's next move.

"Woah, Skylar! Wait-" I start to protest, but it's too late.

With a deafening roar, the combine harvester awakes, its blades whirring to life with deadly precision. Before I can react, my hand is caught in the mechanism, the sharp edges slicing through skin and bone with terrifying speed.

Pain shoots through my hand like a bolt of lightning, and I let out a cry of agony as blood gushes from the wound. Skylar's eyes widen in horror as she realises what she's done, shutting it off immediately; her hands flying to her mouth in shock.

"Dean, oh my God, I'm so sorry!" she cries, her voice trembling with guilt.

Gritting my teeth against the pain, I manage to pry my mangled hand free from the machine's grasp. Blood drips onto the barn floor in a steady rhythm, pooling at my feet as I struggle to regain my composure. The reality of the situation sinks in quickly. I've lost the tops of two fingers, and the pain is excruciating.

I watch, my vision swimming, as Skylar jumps down and hurries to my side.

"Fuck, fuck, fuck!" she panics, looking around. My heart pounds in my chest as I watch her frantically rummaging through dusty crates and old machinery, her movements swift and determined. With trembling hands, she reaches for some old cloth, tearing it into makeshift bandages. "Here," she says, her voice trembling slightly as she kneels beside me and begins wrapping the cloth around my injured fingers; her hands are surprisingly steady. I clench my jaw against the pain as Skylar ties off the makeshift tourniquet, her expression tight with worry.

After Skylar wraps the cloth around my injured fingers, she sits back on her heels, her expression heavy with guilt. I can see the tears welling up in her eyes, threatening to spill over.

"Hey," I say softly, reaching out to gently touch her arm. "It's okay. It was an accident." She sniffles, wiping away a stray tear with the back of her hand.

"But Dean, I have this terrible feeling that.. all of these things *aren't* accidents."

Her words send a chill down my spine, a nagging suspicion clawing its way to the surface of my mind. I swallow hard, trying to ignore the sinking feeling in the pit of my stomach. To push aside the nagging doubt, the creeping sense of unease that threatens to consume me; but sadly, I can't say I disagree with her.

"Come on," I say, forcing a note of false cheer into my voice. "Let's get back so I can wash this out."

CHAPTER 16:
WINGS & WOODWORK
Sienna

Since we got back from the field, Marcus has been up to something outside. I keep hearing all sorts of thumps and bangs, and honestly, I'm too curious for my own good. Yet meanwhile, here I am, snuggled on the bed with my new butterfly buddy on my chest, admiring Butter's beautiful wings; totally mesmerised by her adorable little antics.

As I watch Butter flit around, I can't help but giggle at her playful movements. It's like she knows exactly how to brighten my day with her whimsical, fluttery charm. With each graceful loop and gentle landing, I feel my heart warming to this tiny creature. Her delicate yellow wings shimmer in the soft daylight, casting colourful patterns across the room that match the joy bubbling up inside me.

"You're so pretty, Miss. Butter," I whisper, reaching out a finger for her to perch on. And just like that, she obliges, her tiny feet tickling my skin as she settles in.

Lost in Butter's enchanting dance, I'm startled when the door creaks open, and Marcus strides in, his chest glistening with sweat, his eyes aglow with triumph. He's shirtless, and his rugged physique is accentuated by the effort he's clearly exerted. There's a triumphant grin on his face and he's carrying something wooden.

"Surprise, beautiful." he says softly as he walks closer. I can't help but beam as Marcus sets down a handmade wooden enclosure with mesh walls on the bedside table. It's even filled with plants and a few rocks sitting on the bottom.

"You made this?" I ask delicately. He nods briefly and wipes the glistening sweat from his brow. "It's amazing. I love it." I exclaim, my eyes sparkling with joy as I admire the wooden enclosure. It's clear that he poured his heart and soul into crafting it, and the thoughtfulness behind his gesture warms me to my core.

With a smile, I gently coax Butter onto my finger and guide her into her new home. She flutters around for a moment before settling on a small, wonky perch, her wings beating softly as she explores her new surroundings. Marcus chuckles softly, his eyes glowing with affection as he watches my reaction.

"I'm glad you like it, sweet." he says, his voice tender.

Without a word, I jump to my feet, wrapping my arms around his neck and pulling him into a passionate kiss. Marcus freezes for a moment, clearly caught off guard by my sudden display of affection, but soon melts into the embrace, his arms wrapping around my neck and cheek as he returns the kiss with equal fervour.

Our lips move together in a sweet symphony of love and longing, each kiss filled with the unspoken promise of a future together; Butter fluttering happily in her enclosure next to us.

And at this moment, I know I'm exactly where I'm meant to be.

With a soft moan, I pull Marcus closer, my fingers tangling in his hair as I lose myself in the sensation of his lips on mine. His touch sets my skin ablaze, sending shivers of pleasure racing down my spine. I arch into him, craving more of his touch, more of his love.

Marcus' response is fervent, his lips burning with an intensity that leaves me gasping as he maps every curve of my body. His lips trail down my neck, marking me. As he trails his lips along the curve of my throat, I tilt my head back, offering him access to my neck; my breath quickening.

His hand moves slowly, purposefully up my thigh. The fabric of my dress whispering against my skin as he inches closer to my core. With a gentle touch, he teases the soft skin of my inner thigh, lightly tracing patterns. As I gasp in pleasure, my body responding to his every touch, Marcus continues his sweet torture, slowly inching his hand closer and closer to my pulsating heat. I bite my lip, feeling the dampness between my thighs grow as he continues to tease me through my knickers. His fingers play with the fabric as he whispers in my ear.

"*Fuck*, sweet. You're so wet already. You want it badly, huh?" I look up at him, my eyes wide and needy, as I give a subtle nod. He kisses my forehead before continuing his whispers into my temple. "Not yet, I want you to ache for me." My breath hitches as his fingers graze the sensitive skin of my inner thigh once again, torturously light and deliberate.

I arch my back, pushing my hips towards his hand, silently begging for his touch to move higher. But

Marcus doesn't give in to my silent begging. Instead, he continues to draw out the sweet torture. With a whimper of frustration, I cling to him, my body trembling with need. Marcus leans in, his breath hot against my ear as he murmurs.

"Good girl, so patient."

Just as I think I can't take it anymore, he finally gives in to my silent plea, his fingers slipping past the fabric of my knickers and finding the wet heat waiting for him. Marcus continues to torment me, his fingers expertly teasing my clit with devilish precision. He slides his fingers down from my swollen clit and pushes the tip of his finger into me, slowly stretching and filling me with his touch. I gasp at the sensation, the feeling of him penetrating me so intimately. But before I can fully revel in the pleasure, he cruelly withdraws his finger.

"Marcus, please." I plead, to which he chuckles darkly in response.

"*God.* I love hearing you fucking beg for me." Marcus finally stops his teasing and gives in to his own desire, plunging his fingers deep inside me, causing a squeal to leave my lips. He looks at me with a hungry glare, a predatory glint in his eyes that both thrills and terrifies me.

"Is that what you wanted, sweet?" I nod, unable to form words as his fingers continue their aggressive exploration. I cling to him, my nails digging into his back as I lose myself in the carnal pleasure he's providing.

I feel Marcus's hand tighten around my waist with a possessive grip, as his fingers delve deeper. Pushing firmer. Then he switches; his eyes darken suddenly. Without a word, he flips me over onto my stomach, his strong hands holding me firmly in place as he positions himself behind me. His hands move with purpose, sliding down my spine with a steady pressure that makes me arch my back in response.

He holds me down firmly, his touch demanding as he enters me with a rough thrust. I grip the sheets tightly, my knuckles stretching as I brace myself. Each thrust is deep. He's making the most of me. As Marcus' thrusts grow more intense, I can't help but cry out. I bury my face into the pillow, muffling my moans as he uses me relentlessly.

I swallow hard, my heart pounding in my chest as I feel his dominance enveloping me like a thick fog. I know I should push him away, reclaim control over my own body, but something inside me yearns to surrender; to let him take me completely. With each punishing thrust, he drives me closer to the edge, his fingers digging deep into my skin. I gasp for air, my chest heaving with each ragged breath. Suddenly, his hand wraps around my throat, his grip tight and unyielding.

I choke back a gasp as his fingers tighten, cutting off my air supply.

"You're mine, you hear me?" he growls, his voice rough and commanding. "Mine to fuck, mine to use. Say it." I nod, but that's not what he wanted. With his other hand he sends a punishing smack to my ass. The crack of skin meeting skin reverberating through the room. The pain, sharp and immediate. "Say it. Use your fucking words, Sienna."

"I'm yours," I manage to cry out, my body trembling. A cruel smirk twists at his lips.

"There you fucking go."

He continues to thrust deep into me, hitting every sweet spot there is. I writhe and whimper beneath him, lost in a whirlwind of pleasure and pain. Marcus's voice cuts through the haze once again.

"You want me to fill your mouth or your cunt, sweet?" Before I can answer, he thrusts into me with a brutal force that steals my breath and mind entirely.

"Marcus, please," I manage to whimper, the words barely escaping my lips.

"Fucking pick one," he snarls, his voice dripping with contempt and impatience. With a trembling breath, I manage to rasp out,

"My mouth.. "

"Dirty little girl," he taunts in my ear. "Get on your fucking knees."

Tears sting at the corners of my eyes as I comply, kneeling to the floor beside him, but he walks further away and sits at the dining chair. He pats his leg twice to summon me over.

"Crawl." he commands, "Eyes on me."

Excuse me, sir?

I crawl towards him on my hands and knees, the cold, hard floor scraping against my skin as I move closer; the anticipation and fear building in my chest with every inch I cover. His presence looms over me, casting a dark shadow that engulfs me in a mix of nerves and arousal. My eyes glued up at him. His smile grows with every movement.

"*Fuck*, look at those pretty eyes."

When I finally reach him, he grabs a handful of my hair in a tight grip, pulling me closer to him. His other hand forces his throbbing cock into my unsuspecting mouth, the taste of him overpowering my senses. I gag and choke, the pressure in my chest building as he holds my nose, controlling my breathing with cold calculation. His movements are quick and unforgiving as he uses me for his own pleasure. His grip on my hair tightens, guiding me as I struggle to accommodate his length.

"Take all of it, sweet. Remember, you asked for this." he growls, "Now open nice and wide and choke on my fucking cock." The desire is evident in his voice as he plunges deep down my throat. Each thrust pushes me further into a state of helpless submission. I can only whimper around him, unable to respond as he dominates me completely. The taste of him mingling on my tongue.

With a sudden slap to my face, Marcus' command cuts through the haze of sensation. "I don't want to feel your fucking teeth," he barks, his voice harsh "Suck on it. I want it deep down that little throat." I comply, focusing on relaxing my jaw and throat as I take him as deep as I can, trying to please him just as he demands. The tears streaming down my face mix with the saliva dripping down my chin as he continues to thrust forcefully, using my mouth as his personal playground.

I eagerly obey his command, taking his throbbing cock as deep as I can as he nears his climax. With a primal groan, Marcus' hips jerk forward, and he spills himself into my mouth, filling me with come. Before I can catch my breath, Marcus' hand reaches out, gripping my nose tightly and cutting off my oxygen once again.

"Come on, sweet. Make me proud." he purrs, "swallow every last fucking drop." The taste of him lingers in my mouth, the sensation overwhelming as I struggle to swallow without being able to draw in a breath through my nose. With every ounce of my being, I force myself to swallow, the sensation of his release beginning to slide down my throat.

"That's it," he praises, "Keep going. You're doing so well for me."

As I finally manage to swallow every last drop, a sense of relief washes over me. Taking in a deep breath as Marcus releases his grip on my nose, I gasp for air, feeling his pleasure at my compliance radiating through the room. He pulls up his tracksuit bottoms and settles again onto the edge of the dining chair.

As Marcus leans forwards, he holds my chin in a firm grip, his eyes bore into mine with ferocious intensity. A smirk plays on his lips as he takes in the dishevelled state I'm in; flushed cheeks, heavy breaths, and a wanton look in my eyes.

"Look at the mess I've got you in." He husks, his tone smouldering with desire. "You're dripping for me, aren't you?" I don't reply. He already knows the answer.

"Spread your legs wide, sweet. Let me see you."

As I spread my legs in front of him, Marcus' eyes narrow with a predatory glint. He smirks at the sight of me, exposed and wet.

"Touch yourself, beautiful." he orders, his voice filled with a softer yet commanding authority. Reluctantly, I slowly lower my hand towards the sensitive flesh between my legs, my movements hesitant and uncertain; maintaining eye contact with him as he towers over me.

His eyes narrow with a cruel intensity, a smirk playing on his lips as he takes in the sight of my rising vulnerability. I begin to circle my clit slowly, feeling my wetness on my fingertips; soft whimpers leaving my mouth. His gaze is a piercing force, relentless and unyielding as it rakes over my exposed skin with a primal, hunger-driven intensity that makes my skin prickle with awareness.

"Spread that pussy wider. I wanna see everything." Marcus growls. I comply with Marcus' commands, my legs trembling as I spread myself open for his inspection. My breath hitches at the intimacy of his gaze, his eyes never leaving mine as he takes in the display of my submission. His enjoyment is palpable, his arousal evident in the way his cock strains against the fabric of his joggers.

"Good girl," he murmurs, his voice low and husky with arousal. "Now, put two fingers deep inside for me." I pause, my stare imploring him as I consider whether or not to obey, my fingers trembling with anticipation. But then I surrender, my body responding to the unspoken command as I ease two fingers in, feeling the velvet tightness enveloping them; a soft moan escaping my lips.

"*Fuck*. So pretty when you obey me. All filled and stretched." he murmurs, his voice low and husky with arousal. "Deeper." he commands, his eyes blazing with desire as he watches me comply, sinking my fingers as far as they'll go, seeking out that elusive spot of pleasure deep within me. I gasp at the overwhelming sensation, pleasure coursing through my veins like wildfire. His hands clench, trying to suppress his bulge.

"Soak your clit, now. Let me see how wet you are." He instructs, his voice a husky whisper, flustering me entirely. I slide up my fingers and begin to circle my swollen clit, coating it in my own slick arousal. Marcus watches with hungry eyes, a smirk playing on his lips.

"Such a good girl," he murmurs, his voice laced with approval. "You know just how to please me now, don't you, sweet? How to make yourself all wet and needy." I moan at his words, feeling a rush of heat pooling between my legs at the praise and the degradation mingling together.

"You have my permission, sweet. Now, come for me." With his permission ringing in my ears, I allow myself to succumb fully to the building ecstasy. My movements become more frantic, more desperate as I chase the release he's granted me. Each deep stroke, each touch sends shockwaves of pleasure through me, driving me closer and closer to the edge.

His eyes gleam with primal hunger as I writhe and moan under his command.

"That's it, beautiful. Let me hear you whimper as you fall apart for me." he taunts, his voice thick. The slick sounds of my wetness mixing with the heavy breathing fill the room. My movements become erratic, desperate as I feel the pressure building, the tension coiling tighter and tighter within me. With one final, desperate push, I shatter into million pieces, waves of pleasure crashing over me like a tsunami. I cry out, lost in the overwhelming sensation of release.

Marcus' dark eyes become even more predatory, a low growl slipping from his lips as he watches me fall apart for him. As I collapse in a trembling heap before him, Marcus leans down, his lips brushing against my ear as he whispers,

"Such a good girl. Look at you, all used up and desperate for more."

With a gentle touch, Marcus lifts me from the floor, cradling me in his strong arms as if I were his most precious treasure.

Well, In the most humble way possible, I think I am.

I nestle against his chest, feeling the steady rhythm of his heartbeat beneath my ear, a comforting reassurance of his presence. He holds me close, his warmth enveloping me like a protective shield. His hand strokes my back in soothing circles.

You did so well, sweet" he whispers, his voice soft and filled with tenderness. "I'm so proud of you." I snuggle closer to him, feeling his warmth seeping into my skin.

He suddenly squeezes me extra tightly, spinning me around in his arms before pressing firm, eager kisses to my neck. I gasp in surprise, laughter bubbling up.

"What's with all the excitement?" I ask, trying to sound nonchalant despite the flutter in my chest. He pulls back just enough to lock eyes with me, a mischievous grin spreading across his face like a sunrise.

"Nothing, it's just.. If my younger self could be here now, he wouldn't fucking believe what he's seeing." I blink, struck by the sincerity in his words.

"What do you mean?" I whisper, feeling a lump form in my throat. I can't help but beam from ear to ear, my face aching with the force of my smile. Marcus' chuckle is a low, gentle hum, his eyes sparkling with love and adoration as they drink in the sight of me.

"Sienna, I don't think you realise. You're literally all I've ever wanted."

I meet his stare, feeling a rush of warmth spread through me at the depth of his words. My heart flutters in my chest as I listen, unable to tear my eyes away from him. He brushes his thumb against my cheek,

"You're the only person I can soften up around, sweet. You're a constant." he says, his voice filled with a quiet sincerity. "When everything in my life is continuously changing, you're the one thing that remains the same." I find myself at a loss for words, my heart overflowing with emotions. Unable to find the right words to express how I feel, I simply gaze into Marcus' eyes, my own eyes welling up with tears.

"I'd do anything to spend the rest of my life just curled up with you in your little bubble," he continues, his voice soft yet strong with conviction. "Where regardless of everything you're put through, you act like the world is full of rainbows and unicorns, and everything tastes like strawberries."

I can't help but smile, a soft, gentle curve of my lips, as I bask in the glow of his love and devotion. A rush of warmth floods through my veins, leaving me tingling from head to toe.

It's like I'm floating on a cloud.

"You know what's funny?" I reply, timidly "I love that you remind me that the world isn't all rainbows and unicorns."

Marcus chuckles, the sound vibrating against my skin as he continues to hold me close. His laughter is infectious. Wrapping my arms around him, I bury my face in his chest, feeling his warmth envelop me like a cocoon.

And In this moment, I know that I'm exactly where I belong

CHAPTER 17:
LOST LEADS

Dean

Marcus and I bundle into the car, the engine growling to life as we set our sights on Moth. Marcus' eyes flick to my hand, his brow furrowing in concern.

"What's up with your hand?" he asks. I let out a defeated sigh, my grip on the wheel tightening.

"It doesn't matter." I mutter, lacking the energy to explain. "So, Moth," I grunt, "you think he's gonna play nice?"

Marcus smirks, his eyes scanning the passing scenery with a steely gaze.

"I doubt it."

He reaches into his pocket and pulls out a joint.

"You want a hit?" he offers casually. I hesitate for a moment before taking the joint from him, indulging in a quick drag. As I exhale, I glance at Marcus.

"You think we smoke too much?" I ask in a half-serious tone. Marcus chuckles, exhaling a cloud of smoke.

"For the shit we've been through, I don't think we smoke enough." I smirk at Marcus's response, shaking my head in amusement.

"Fair point," I concede. Marcus takes another long drag, his expression thoughtful as he exhales a plume of smoke out the window.

I glance over at Marcus, noticing the relaxed demeanour he's sporting.

"You don't seem too worried about these guys," I remark, raising an eyebrow. Marcus lets out a low chuckle, a smirk playing on his lips.

"Dean, you gave me a fucking gun. You realise I'm like invincible now," he says with mock seriousness, his ego seemingly inflated. I know he's always been into weapons. Far more than I am. His collection of knives is ever-growing and I suppose I should've guessed that giving him a gun was quite the step up.

"It'd be great if it worked like that, huh?"

As we pull up to the location, I spot a very large, muscular figure standing outside, puffing away at a cigarette. Tattoos cover his body and face; but not the cool kind of tattoos, the really shitty kind of tattoos. He looks like the type of person you wouldn't fuck with. Instinct tells me it's Moth. We exchange a glance, and without a word, Marcus and I decide to observe from the other side of the street through our tinted windows. We sit and we watch.

But before we can make a move, his sharp glare catches sight of our car, and he immediately senses something's amiss. With a quick pivot, he strides purposefully a few paces down an alleyway, disappearing and reappearing in a car. I gun the engine, peeling out from our hiding spot and tearing after him. As we chase him through the labyrinth of streets, the car's tires screech against the asphalt. Marcus grips the grab handle, his knuckles white with tension, while I focus on keeping us on his tail.

Just as we start to gain ground, I can't help but notice the number plate on the car, 'M0TH M4N' The arrogance of it makes me smirk. Marcus catches my eye, a silent acknowledgment passing between us. I'll give it to him, It's a bold move, broadcasting your identity like that when there's probably a lot of fuckers wanting him dead.

As the pursuit intensifies, Moth leads us into a part of town we know all too well from our upbringing. The streets grow narrower, the buildings taller and more dilapidated. It's the kind of place where trouble lurks around every corner.

Suddenly, Moth's car cuts sharply into a narrow alley, and we follow, adrenaline pumping. But as we emerge on the other side, his vehicle suddenly screeches to a halt, wedging us in place. The abrupt halt leaves us momentarily disoriented.

Before we can react, the sound of unanticipated gunfire fills the air, bullets raining down on us from Moth's car. Marcus and I duck for cover, the car's windows shattering under the onslaught. We grit our teeth, scrambling for our weapons as we desperately return fire. But as we exchange shots, it becomes painfully clear that Moth's not alone. Shadows move in the back of his car, indicating he's got backup.

"Bro, we've got no fucking chance!" Marcus shouts, his voice strained with urgency as he squeezes off a few rounds in Moth's direction.

My mind races as I weigh our options. We're outnumbered and outgunned, and staying put is a death sentence.

"Stay down!" I bark, my voice strained with determination; barely audible over the chaos. Bullets whiz past us, kicking up puffs of dust as we move, the adrenaline coursing through our veins.

I slam the gear into reverse, the tires screeching as we peel out of the alley, narrowly avoiding another barrage of bullets. As we speed away, I spare a glance at Marcus. His jaw is set in a grim line.

"Fucking bastards," he growls, his voice low and menacing. I nod in agreement, my own anger bubbling to the surface.

"Oh, don't worry. If they wanna play fucking dirty, we will too."

CHAPTER 18:

TAKEN

Sienna

7:43 p.m. Marcus has been gone for a while, but thankfully, the gentle presence of Butter has stopped the boredom. Her wings flutter softly, dancing around me; a vibrant splash of colour against the dimly lit room.

With a soft giggle, I lift my head from the pillow and reach for the slice of juicy orange that sits on my bedside table, holding it out like a precious gift. Butter lands on my finger with the grace of a ballerina, her tiny legs brushing against my skin as she nibbles on the sweet treat.

"Do you like oranges, Miss. Butter?" I whisper, my heart swelling with love as she dances around in delight.

As Butter continues to flit around me, her movements grow increasingly erratic, and a sense of unease creeps over me.

"What's wrong, Butter?" I ask softly, my voice tinged with concern as I watch her fluttering about in a frenzy. But before I can register what's happening, the peaceful serenity of the moment shatters into chaos as the door bursts open with a deafening crash. Four menacing figures, clad in black hoodies and masks, storm into the room and straight at me with ruthless efficiency.

My heart pounds in my chest as fear grips me, paralysing me for a moment. But instinct kicks in, and I let out a piercing scream, my voice echoing off the walls as I fight against the hands that grab at me. With desperate strength, I struggle against my assailants, clawing and kicking in a frantic bid for freedom.

"Let me go! Please!" I plead. But their grip is unyielding, and a sharp blow sends searing pain coursing through me, causing stars to dance before my eyes.

"Shut the fuck up." one of them laughs, his voice cold and menacing.

Blood spurts from my lip and I'm greeted by the bitter taste of iron, but I refuse to give in, fighting with every fibre of my being. Through the haze of pain and panic, I catch a glimpse of Butter, fluttering in confusion as she lands in a pool of crimson. As I'm dragged away, my fingernails scrape against the floor, my desperate fingers flailing wildly in a futile attempt to grasp hold of anything that might grant me a fleeting chance of freedom. The sound of my own ragged breathing echoes through my mind as I'm pulled inexorably towards the door.

Salt-stung tears stream down my face, blurring my vision and rendering the world around me a hazy, indistinct mess. I let out a raw, anguished cry, my desperation echoing through the air.

"Marcus!" But my cries fall on deaf ears, drowned out by the cruel laughter and taunts of my captors.

"Your little boyfriend can't save you now, sweetheart," one of them sneers.

How dare the word 'sweet' even leave his ugly fucking mouth.

Then the tallest one chimes in, his words laced with venom.

"Your friends should have known better than to mess with us, princess. Now you're gonna pay the fucking price." *The price for what?* Amidst the chaos, I glance around and notice the others looking to him, as if seeking approval or direction. Each word cuts deeper than the last, a cruel reminder of the danger I'm in. But even as fear grips me, I refuse to give up hope.

Another voice joins in, equally sinister.

"She's putting up quite the fight, boss," he chuckles, addressing the tallest man with a tone of reverence. I watch him survey me with a cold gaze. His eyes eerily the same colour as Marcus'.

"Yeah, she's a feisty one, that's for sure," he replies, his voice carrying a dangerous edge.

With every ounce of strength I have left, I continue to struggle against my captors, my cries of defiance echoing through the night. But as they drag me further and further away from safety, the darkness closes in around me. My struggles grow more frantic, but the iron grasp of my captors holds firm, inexorably propelling me towards the sinister silhouette of a black car, its very presence seeming to draw all lingering moonlight out of the air. I pay attention to the number plate, not that I even know how it will possibly help me now; 'M0TH M4N'

I prefer butterflies, fuckface.

As I'm bundled into the boot, the same sense of dread washes over me, the memory of this same black car following me days before flooding back with chilling clarity. It's a grim realisation that crashes down on me like a hammer blow; I've been caught in the snare of those who have been stalking me, and now I'm trapped, at their mercy.

The boot lid crashes down, a metallic slap that reverberates through my eardrums, like a guillotine blade falling. The sound waves resonate through my body, sending a shiver of dread coursing down my spine, as I'm trapped in the dark, airless tomb of the car. The metal presses against my skin, cold and unforgiving, as if it's trying to crush the life out of me.

We speed off into the unknown, and my mind races with a million thoughts and fears. What do they want with me? Where are they taking me? And most importantly, is Marcus okay?

As the engine dies, the silence is oppressive, my heart racing in tandem; uncertain of what's waiting for me outside this car. The boot suddenly swings open, and I'm roughly pulled out of the car, my feet stumbling on the ground as they cover my mouth and drag me towards a looming house. I find myself in the middle of nowhere, surrounded by darkness that stretches as far as the eye can see. The house before us seems out of place in this desolate landscape, its silhouette stark against the night sky.

As the men force me inside, I realise the interior of the house is not what I had expected. It's messy, cluttered with the detritus of daily life, but there's an eerie sense of emptiness to it, as if no one truly lives here except for the occasional visitor.

Down we go, deeper into the bowels of the house until we reach a basement. It's dank and musty, the air heavy with the scent of neglect. The walls seem to be slowly surrendering to the relentless creep of dampness; the floor littered with discarded items. There are two rooms down here. One door is locked tight, its presence ominous.

My captors push me into the other room, the darkness swallowing me whole. There are no windows, no lights, just a bed in the centre of the room. Thrown onto the cold, hard ground, I gasp for air as they yank off their masks and pull down their hoods. My eyes dart wildly around the room, trying to commit each face to memory. But it's like trying to grasp a handful of sand; the features blur together as I struggle to process the horror before me. I focus. I focus *hard*.

The first man is a behemoth, his massive muscles bulging beneath his hoodie like a grotesque parody of human form. A tattoo slashes across his cheek, a cruel smile twisting his lips as he leers at me with a calculating gaze.

The second man is a scrawny figure, his face contorted in a sadistic grin as he watches my struggles with an air of morbid fascination. His eyes seem to gleam with an unholy excitement.

The third man stands tall and imposing, his features obscured in darkness. The only noticeable feature being his large, black beard, like a shadowy halo. Exuding an air of authority, his presence commanding respect from the others.

And then there's *him*, the tallest one, his presence looming over me like a dark storm cloud. There's something about him that makes my skin crawl.

He's handsome.
I think it's his smile.

Charming, with deeply sunk dimples on both of his cheeks.

No, it's his eyes; cold and calculating, but the same fucking hazel colour as Marcus'.
I hate him instantly.

He takes a deliberate step forward, his movements calculated and menacing, as he drops to one knee in front of me. his glare locks on mine as he reaches out to caress my cheek with a chilling familiarity.

"Pretty little thing, aren't you, princess?" I recoil from his touch, his resemblance to Marcus sending waves of disgust through my body.

As he turns to the others, his voice cold and commanding, I know what's coming next.

"Strip her." he orders, his gaze never leaving mine as the others move to obey his command. And in that moment, as their hands reach for me,

I know that my nightmare has only just begun.

CHAPTER 19:
THE WORST THING POSSIBLE

Marcus

After a few hours of joyriding, in an attempt to clear our heads, Dean eases the car to a stop outside the cottage; a small sense of contentment washing over us. But as he kills the engine and I glance towards the cottage, that contentment evaporates in an instant.

"Hold on," I mutter, my eyes scanning the surroundings with a sense of unease.

The door, usually sturdy and secure, is now hanging off its hinges, splintered wood scattered across the ground. My heart lurches into my throat, and a cold sweat breaks out on the back of my neck.

"Oh, fuck," I whisper under my breath, my pulse quickening and dread settling like a heavy weight in my gut.

Without waiting for a second thought, I'm out of the car and charging towards the cottage, my footsteps heavy and urgent. Every worst-case scenario unfolds in vivid detail in my mind's eye as I step inside, Dean following close behind. As Dean mutters, "Shit." under his breath, a sinking feeling settles in the pit of my stomach. The sight of blood staining the floor sends a wave of visceral horror and anguish crashing over me, threatening to drown out all rational thought.

My heart clenches painfully in my chest, each beat echoing like a drum of despair. "No," I whisper, the word barely audible over the pounding in my ears. The realisation hits me like a freight train and the guilt is suffocating, choking me with a relentless grip.

My legs tremble beneath me, unable to support my weight; my knees buckling beneath the crushing weight of despair as I crouch to the floor. The sight of crimson staining the floor is like a knife to the heart; each drop a painful poke in my side, tormenting me with thoughts of the danger she's in.

But then, I catch sight of Butter, her delicate wings now smeared with the same red hue. The memory of Sienna's warm laughter and gentle touch as she played with Butter flashes before me, filling the room with a sense of warmth and light. The thought of her, so innocent and sweet, torn from us in such a brutal way is almost too much to bear. Where could she be? What unspeakable horrors are being inflicted upon her? My thoughts spin into a maddening vortex. A complete frenzy.

With a guttural growl, I rise to my feet, the sight of Butter triggering a torrent of rage. My hand lashes out, striking the wall with a resounding thud as I curse under my breath. The wall folding around my cut knuckles.

"Fuck!" I roar, the sound echoing around the room like thunder. Without another word, I storm out of the room. "Go check on Sky, now!" I order.

"Bro, wait, we need to think this through-" Dean's voice cuts through the haze of my anger, but I don't stop.

"Now!" I bark, my tone laced with a lethal edge. "I'm not fucking around." There's a tiny moment of hesitation in Dean's eyes, a flicker of uncertainty. But then he nods, the gravity of the situation dawning on him. "Okay, okay," he says, his voice firm. "I'll go get her. Just breathe, man. Please." I turn away, my mind consumed by a single, burning thought.

*I won't rest until every single cunt who laid a hand on her is **dead.***

CHAPTER 20:

HELP

Sienna

My heart races as the men advance, their movements predatory, like wolves closing in on their prey. I scramble backward, my hands searching desperately for something, anything to defend myself with, but finding nothing but empty space.

The first man grabs at my shirt, ripping it open with a forceful tug. I feel a surge of panic, a primal instinct to fight back rising within me, but I know deep down that resistance would be futile against their overwhelming strength. Tears sting my eyes as they strip away my dignity along with my clothes. I close my eyes, trying to block out the horror unfolding around me, but their taunts and jeers seep through, haunting me like a nightmare from which I cannot wake.

I try to scream, but my voice catches in my throat, choked off by fear and disgust. I can feel their eyes on me, leering with a sickening hunger that makes my skin crawl. Panic grips me as they pin me down on my back. The hard, unforgiving surface of this sad excuse for a bed, pushing into my spine; their weight crushing me beneath them.

With rough hands, they pin my legs up by my side, exposing me completely to their depraved eyes. A wave of loathing and desperation crashes over me as they loom closer, their malevolent intent palpable in the air.

"*Shit*, look at that," one man grunts, his voice thick with malice, his calloused hand grabbing at my ass, squeezing it roughly.

"Yeah, we're gonna have fun with this one."

"Please," I whimper, the word barely more than a whisper as tears stream down my face, mingling with the sweat that coats my skin. But they pay no heed to my pleas, their hands roaming over my body with greedy anticipation.

"You scared, princess?" The tall one taunts. I remain frozen, staring into him with sick intensity.

"Don't worry, you'll learn to love it." He states as he touches me; colder and more calculated than the others. He watches me with a predatory gleam in his eyes, his fingers trailing lightly over my skin as if savouring the sensation of my helplessness. Their laughter filling the room like a noxious gas.

I feel a sickening knot form in the pit of my stomach as one of them takes out his penis, the sight of it making me want to retch. Before plunging into me, he utters,

"Let's see how much fight you've got, sweetheart." Every fibre of my being screams in protest as he moves closer, his eyes gleaming with malicious intent. I struggle against their grasp, but it's futile. They overpower me easily, their strength too much for me to overcome.

Marcus. All I want is Marcus.

…Unaware that I had even closed them, I open my eyes. Fuck, I must have passed out. Pain radiates through me as I hit the floor, the cold surface biting into my skin like icy tendrils of despair. I whimper in agony, my senses overwhelmed by the sheer brutality of their actions.

The men crouch down, their hands reaching out to deliver one last punishment. Some of them slap my ass while one slices my thighs with brutal force; another holding me down by my hair. The sting of their blows is like a physical manifestation of their contempt, branding me. And then, one by one, they add insult to injury by spitting on my spent body with contemptuous disdain. Each glob of saliva lands with a sickening splatter.

I lie there, despondent and broken, as they continue their assault, their laughter cutting through me worse than the knife. The room spins with a nauseating haze of pain, each moment stretching into an eternity of suffering. I don't even possess the energy to scream.

"Now, make sure you remember this feeling next time you wanna fucking fight us."

With a glance over their shoulders, they unleash one last volley of contemptuous laughter, the sound reverberating in the confines of the room like a haunting melody of despair. And then, in one swift motion, the leader reaches for the door handle, his fingers curling around it.

The door swings open, flooding the room with harsh, unforgiving light from the corridor beyond. For a moment, I'm blinded by its intensity, entirely disorientated. And then, with a deafening slam, the door is closed, sealing me in darkness once more. I can hear the click of the lock, a final nail in the coffin.

Alone in the mirk, surrounded by the wreckage of their cruelty, I lie there in a tangled mess. Tears stream down my cheeks, mingling with the filth that now stains my skin. I am broken, discarded, left to wallow in the aftermath of their depravity.

Marcus, where are you?

CHAPTER 21:

FIND HER

Dean

"So you're telling me you didn't hear or see anything?" Marcus's voice cuts through the tension in the car, his frustration palpable. Skylar's response is quiet, drowned out by the weight of guilt hanging heavy in the air.

"I had my headphones in," she mumbles, her eyes fixed on the back of the passenger seat.

The admission lands like a punch to the gut, and I feel my own frustration bubbling to the surface. I'm happy she's okay but she was right fucking there, lost in her own world. She missed the whole thing, and now she's useless in helping us find Sienna. I clench my jaw, struggling   to   contain   the   irritation.

"Fuck's sake, Sky." I growl, my voice rough with emotion. "How could you be that fucking oblivious? You're lucky they didn't grab you too."

"I'm sorry, okay! Do you not think I feel bad enough without both of you lecturing me?" Her outburst catches me off guard, the raw emotion in her voice momentarily silencing my anger. I exchange a glance with Marcus, seeing the conflict mirrored in his eyes. We're all on edge, emotions running high in the tense atmosphere of the car.

Marcus's silence speaks volumes, the disappointment thick in his eyes. We all know Skylar fucked us up here, and the thought makes my blood boil, but now's not the time to tear each other apart. I let out a heavy sigh, my shoulders slumping with resignation.

"We can't change what's been done," I mutter, my voice heavy with regret. "Let's just focus on finding her, alright?"

With a nod from Marcus, I turn my attention to the road ahead. But as I glance past him, I notice his knuckles white from gripping the steering wheel so tightly. His jaw is clenched, his eyes locked in place, focused on the dark road like a hawk zeroing in on its prey.

He's driving like a man possessed, his anger and determination fueling every reckless move. The car lurches around corners, accelerates with a roar, and Skylar and I shoot each other a quick, worried glance;

I can practically feel Skylar's fear radiating off her as she grips the door handle tight enough to leave marks. We're all tense, but with Marcus in this state, nobody dares speak up.

Don't poke the Bear.

As we pull up in a screech at the place where we first spotted Moth, the tension in the car reaches a notable peak. Marcus doesn't waste a moment. With a sense of urgency that borders on desperation, he reaches for his gun, readying it with efficiency. The click of the magazine being loaded echoes in the tense silence of the car.

Skylar's hand hovers over the door handle, her expression a map of uncertainty and concern. Her eyes, a deep well of worry, plead for Marcus to slow down and think things through. But Marcus seems oblivious to her silent protest, his focus singular and unwavering. Marcus opens the door and stands up, his movements quick and decisive. I start to speak, wanting to urge caution,

"Bro, just wait a minute-" but before I can finish, he cuts me off with a sharp slam of the door.

As Marcus practically runs towards the warehouse, my heart sinks like a stone in my chest. I let out a heavy sigh, frustration and worry mingling in the pit of my stomach. With a shake of my head, I reach for my gun. Skylar shoots me a look of concern, her gaze darting to the weapon in my hand as if it's a harbinger of doom. I nod at her once, a brief, reassuring motion

"You stay in here, alright? Call me if you see anything dodgy." She nods.

"Okay," she says softly, her voice wavering slightly. "Be safe."

My mind instantly pans to thoughts of my Delilah as I reply,

"Always."

With a muttered curse under my breath, I follow Marcus, my senses on high alert as we approach the dark alley. Every step feels like walking towards the edge of a cliff, teetering on the brink of disaster. I quicken my pace to catch up to Marcus, who's already swinging open a door down the side of the alley.

My grip tightens around the handle of my gun as we cautiously move forward, our footsteps echoing against the concrete floor. The darkness inside the warehouse swallows us up as we step inside, the air thick with the smell of weed and motor oil. The dim street lights filter through the dusty windows and cast long shadows across the floor.

Rows of shelves line the walls, stacked high with boxes and crates; full to the brim with packaged drugs. And as my gaze lands on the rows of expensive cars parked neatly on the far side of the room, I understand that this isn't just a simple warehouse; it's a base of operations, a hub for Moth and his cronies.

I exchange a tense glance with Marcus, the weight of our mission bearing down on us like a heavy burden. We need to find Sienna, and fast. But as we move deeper into the warehouse, it becomes increasingly clear that Moth and his crew are nowhere to be found. Our frustration boils over, the anger and stress mingling into a potent cocktail of emotions. We came here for answers, for revenge, but all we're left with is an empty warehouse and more questions than ever.

Without a word, Marcus lets out a built up force of anger, his fists swinging wildly as he starts wrecking boxes, his movements fueled by raw fury. I stand frozen, my jaw dropped in stunned silence, as he swings the butt of his gun with reckless abandon, smashing the car windows into a kaleidoscope of shattered glass and twisted metal. The sound of shattering glass and his screams of frustration echo through the empty space, tearing at my soul like claws. Each blow is a release of pent-up frustration. He's in so much pain, and all I can do is watch him fall apart.

But as the reality sinks in that time is ticking, and we're no closer to Sienna, Marcus's rage turns into something darker. He collapses to his knees, a primal sound escaping his throat, raw and gut-wrenching. It's as if he's been torn apart from the inside. I stumble to his side, my heart shattering into a million pieces at the sight of his devastation.

"Bro," I choke out, my voice cracking with emotion. "We're gonna find her, I know we are." But he doesn't respond, his whole being consumed by a darkness so profound it's suffocating. It's like he's been stripped to the bone by the cruel hand of fate.

Marcus mutters under his breath,

"*God*, what are they doing to her?" I can see the torment etched on his face, the fear and anguish twisting his features as he imagines the worst possible scenarios for Sienna. It's like he's being cursed by his own nightmares, unable to escape the incessant grip of his own imagination.

I glance at Marcus, and the agony etched on his face cuts me deeper than any blade ever could. His eyes are haunted, filled with tears he refuses to shed.

"Don't," I rasp, "Don't you dare even think about it." But Marcus's empty leer betrays the depths of his torment, his mind a battleground of horrors too terrible to contemplate.

It's as if he's already lost her.

As the weight of our failure presses down on us like a suffocating shroud, we resign ourselves to the bitter truth; tonight, there's nothing left for us to do.

CHAPTER 22:

NOAH

Sienna

As I lie there on the cold floor, still reeling from the agony of the assault, the passage of time blurs into a painful haze; and as early morning rays of sunlight creep through the cracks, I soon realise it's the next day.

The oppressive silence is shattered by the faint creak of the door hinges, and a sliver of light spills into the room. My heart pounds in my chest as I watch the leader step inside, a plate of food in hand. He doesn't speak, doesn't offer any words of comfort or remorse. Instead, he simply sits on the edge of the bed, his presence a menacing shadow.

With a callous disregard for my suffering, he places the plate of food on the floor before me, his gaze cold and indifferent.

"Eat," he commands, his voice devoid of any warmth. It's a command, plain and simple. But I can't bring myself to comply, not after everything they've done to me.

"I don't trust it," I whisper, the words barely escaping my trembling lips. Every fibre of my being screams at me to resist, to reject whatever he's presenting me with. But the hunger beginning to poke at my insides threatens to override my instincts, reminding me of my desperate need for sustenance. He chuckles darkly, a cold smile twisting his lips.

"I've killed a lot of people, princess." His tone is icy, like death itself. "And I'll have you know, poisoning is by far the most boring method there is," he continues, his voice lowering to a sinister whisper. "If I wanted you dead, I would've slit your fucking throat. Eat."

The words hit me like a physical blow, knocking the breath from my lungs. The sheer brutality of his statement leaves me reeling, my mind struggling to process the horror of what he's just said. I stare at the food, my stomach churning with revulsion.

How can I even think about eating?

But a deep-seated instinct for survival urges me to obey, to consume whatever morsel of sustenance I can find in this place. With trembling hands, I reach for the plate, my fingers brushing against the hot surface. As I lift the first mouthful of food to my lips, I can feel his eyes boring into me. Each movement feels like a betrayal of everything I stand for, but in this hellhole, defiance only leads to more pain.

Despite my initial hesitation, I tentatively take a bite of the food, expecting the worst. But to my surprise, it's not the tasteless gruel I anticipated. It's warm, comforting even. But beneath its soothing heat, a cold dread simmers, a creeping sense of unease that refuses to be stilled. It's as if the warmth is a fragile truce, one that can't begin to dispel the dark suspicions that gnaw at my gut. This kindness feels like a cruel trick, a prelude to more suffering.

But as I take another bite, I push those thoughts aside, if only for a moment, allowing myself to savour this small semblance of normalcy.

As I finish the last bite of the surprisingly palatable meal, the leader's voice cuts through once again.

"How was it?" His tone is deceptively casual, almost conversational. I hesitate, unsure of how to respond to his unexpected inquiry.

"It was.. fine." I finally manage to choke out. He chuckles darkly,

"Good, good. I'm glad you enjoyed it."

For a moment, we're locked in a tense silence, each of us sizing the other up, trying to gauge the other's intentions. As we lock eyes, a strange sense of curiosity washes over me. I can't help but notice how handsome he is, how clean, how.. normal; his features chiselled and sharp. He couldn't be much older than me, I realise, a fact that only adds to the mystery surrounding him. As his eyes wander, I'm suddenly acutely aware of my vulnerable state that I had almost forgotten, entirely naked in front of him.

"What's your name, princess?" I hesitate for a moment, my mind racing. Should I tell him? Does it even matter?

"Sienna,"

He nods, as if filing away the information for future use. "What's yours?" I find myself asking, unable to stop the words from escaping my lips. He smiles genuinely, his dimples deep; as if he'd never been asked a question before.

"Noah." he replies simply. He looks at me with purpose, his eyes locked in place.

"So, *Sienna*, what's your favourite meal? I'll make it for you later." I should probably be feeling more disturbed about my captor's sudden interest in my favourite food, but I'm honestly more taken aback by the fact that he took the time to cook the meal himself.

"You cooked this?" The words escape my lips in a hushed whisper; disbelief mingling with a tinge of curiosity as I glance at the plate before me. Noah's lips curve into a faint smirk, a glint of pride dancing in his eyes.

"Yes, princess. Surprised?" His tone holds a hint of mockery, as though my astonishment amuses him. I nod slowly, unable to tear my focus away from him, still trying to process. "My mother taught me how to cook." Noah continues, his voice softening slightly as he speaks of his mother.

For an instant, the mask of indifference cracks. There's a flicker of humanity in his eyes, a glimpse of the person he might have been before whatever the fuck happened to lead him here.

"She sounds nice," I offer tentatively. A shadow passes over Noah's features, his gaze distant.

"She was," he murmurs, his voice tinged with melancholy. "She's dead." The silence that follows is heavy with unspoken pain, and I can feel the weight of my own grief settling in my chest.

"I understand." I offer softly, my throat tight with emotion. He raises an eyebrow, urging me to elaborate. "Both of my parents are dead too," I confess, the words spilling forth before I can stop them.

For a moment, a flicker of understanding passes between us, a shared sorrow that transcends the boundaries of the situation. In that instant, the walls that separate us seem to crumble; a strange kinship in our shared loss. Noah's expression softens with genuine empathy.

"I'm sorry, Sienna." he says, his voice carrying a weight of sincerity that catches me off guard.

"It's okay."

I find myself unable to tear my eyes away from him, captivated by the terrifying intensity of his stare. In his eyes, I see a reflection of my own insecurities.

"Why am I here?" I ask, avoiding any continuation of the current topic. Noah gives a sinister grin.

"Your little friend, Dean. And his mates," he starts, "they've got you into quite a bit of trouble."

"What did he do?"

"I wish I knew exactly," he says, "Despite what people think, Grizzly doesn't tell me everything. "

I struggle to find the strength to understand or even process his words. My mind races with questions, but the exhaustion weighs heavy on my limbs, leaving me unable to even muster the energy to ask who Grizzly is.

"Anyway, how are you feeling, princess? Did we rough you up too much?" he asks, his tone strangely calm. I swallow hard, my throat dry and constricted.

"I'm fine." It's a lie, of course, but admitting weakness feels like surrendering.

Without warning, Noah's fingers dig into my arms, his grip like a vice as he hauls me onto my feet. I can't suppress the sharp intake of breath that escapes me.

"I'll be the judge of that." I stagger slightly, my legs threatening to give way beneath me. Noah pays no mind to my struggle, his attention focused solely on my injuries. He runs his hands over my bruised and battered flesh, his touch cold and clinical. But also, strangely gentle.

I flinch as his touch lingers on the most intimate parts of my body, his fingers tracing over the bruises, cuts and marks left behind by their relentless assault.

"Was there much blood when we finished with you?" he asks, his tone disturbingly casual.

"Uh, I don't remember." I mumble, my eyebrows scrunched in confusion.

"It's okay, princess," he says with a straight face, his fingers trailing lightly along the jagged edges of a particularly nasty bruise. "I don't expect you to remember everything."

His words stun me, the contradiction between his gentle and callous words leaving me utterly bewildered. I struggle to comprehend the situation. I struggle to work him out. Why is he even in here doing this? Noah's actions, his alternating between cruel indifference and unsettling care, leave me disorientated and reeling with so many questions.

Then, his hand comes down lightly on my bruised and tender behind; the impact sending a jolt of pain coursing through my body. I gasp, taken aback by the suddenness of the gesture, my muscles tensing in response. My eyes widen in surprise as I process what just happened. It wasn't a harsh or brutal smack, but rather almost casual, as if it were an everyday occurrence.

He chuckles lightly at my reaction.

"You'll live." he jokes with a wink, and in a relaxed yet deliberate motion, he gently shoves me back onto the floor. Though the action isn't rough, the underlying threat lingers in the air, a constant reminder of the power he holds here.

"Hey, what was that for?" I question with a scowl. Noah floods the room with genuine laughter and presenting a charming smile he replies.

"Careful, princess." he taunts, "You're getting too brave."

Noah grabs the plate and stands, his imposing figure casting a shadow over me as he makes a show of straightening his shirt. As he walks and reaches for the door handle, I speak, my voice gentle.

"You're a bad person."

He pauses, his hand hovering over the handle, before slowly turning to face me. A curious glint in his eyes.

"Correct. I am." he admits, his voice low and menacing. "But at least I'm honest about it. Can you say the same about your little friends? After all, they're the reason you're here in the first place, right?"

My breath catches in my throat, a surge of anger rising within me at his cruel insinuation.

"They're nothing like you."

"If that was the case, they wouldn't even be on our radar." he laughs, "And where are they now, princess? Huh? Whilst you're here with me. Lying naked, on the floor. Where are they?" Noah's smirk twists into a sadistic grin as he watches a small hint of doubt dawn on me. "Get some more sleep while you can."

With that, he turns on his heel and strides out of the room,

leaving me alone with my thoughts.

CHAPTER 23:
WHERE IS SHE?

Marcus

The morning light filters through the curtains. I sit at the dining table in Dean's room, my mind racing with a thousand thoughts, yet I feel numb, disconnected from reality. Sienna's absence hangs in the air like a heavy cloud, suffocating me with each passing moment.

I haven't slept at all; the events of last night replaying in my mind like a broken record, each moment etched into my memory with painful clarity.

I can hear the soft sounds of breathing from Dean, a stark contrast to the turmoil raging within me. I feel like a caged animal, restless and on edge, desperate for some semblance of control in a situation spiralling out of hand.

I can't bring myself to move, rooted to the spot. Paralyzed.

I close my eyes, trying to push back the overwhelming tide threatening to drown me. But even in the darkness behind my eyelids, I can still see her face, haunted by a pain I couldn't protect her from. Where the fuck have they taken her? What have they done to her? The thoughts fill me with a cold dread that I can't ignore.

Several more hours pass as I sit there, lost in my thoughts. The minutes crawl by, each one more painful than the last.

When Dean finally stirs around 11 a.m., I'm snapped out of my reverie. His voice drifts from the other room, muted yet comforting in familiarity.

"You up?" he asks through the door.

"Of course I am." Dean enters the room, his expression sombre as he takes in the scene before him. He can see the exhaustion etched into every line of my face, offering me a sympathetic glance before taking a seat opposite me at the table.

"How'd you sleep?" he asks, his voice gentle yet tinged with concern. I meet his gaze, unable to mask the weariness that weighs me down.

"Didn't. Personally I don't know how you could." I snap through gritted teeth. I mean what I say. I feel like I'm on another planet. How any of us could sleep through this is beyond me.

"If we get no sleep we're useless, man."

After a moment of silence, Dean begins to get changed.

"How was Sky?" I ask. He hesitates for a moment, his expression guarded.

"Fine," he says tersely, his voice tight with emotion. "I made sure she blocked her door."

"Good."

As Dean finishes getting changed, I straighten up in my seat, steeling myself for the conversation that I know needs to happen.

"We need to go back to the warehouse," I say, my voice low but determined. "I can't sit around any longer."

"Of course," he replies, his voice heavy, "but we need to take our time, bro. The way you walked in there last night would've gotten us killed, we were *so* unprepared." I feel a surge of frustration at his words, knowing that he's right but hating the feeling in my stomach.

"We don't have time!" I snap, through gritted teeth. "Sienna's out there, God knows where, and we're sitting here twiddling our fucking thumbs! Sleeping!" But Dean doesn't back down.

"I get it, man," he says, his voice steady despite my agitation. "But this is a serious organisation, we can't pile in without some kind of plan. If we get ourselves killed what fucking good are we to Sienna?" I scoff, the sound bitter and mocking.

"A plan?" I repeat incredulously. "And what good has all this cautious planning done so far? Huh?" I retort, my voice tinged with annoyance and worry. "We've been tiptoeing around, playing it safe in these shitty cottages in the middle of nowhere, and where has it gotten us?"

Dean meets my gaze, his expression a mixture of understanding and concern.

"I know you're worried, bro. We all are." he says, his voice calm but tinged with caution. "But we need to think this through." I shake my head, my frustration reaching its peak.

"I've been thinking all fucking night!" I snap, the words bursting from me like a dam breaking under pressure. "Trust me, bro. I've thought of everything."

There's a heavy weight in my chest as I say the words, the reality of what Sienna might be enduring as we speak. I can't bear to think about it, can't bear to imagine the pain and terror she might be experiencing.

But I can't ignore it either, not when her life hangs in the balance.

Without another word, I rise from my seat, the chair scraping against the floor as I push it back with more force than necessary.

"Fuck this." I mutter under my breath, my hand instinctively reaching for my gun. I can't stand the thought of waiting any longer, of letting Sienna suffer while we sit idly by. Dean's eyes widen in alarm as he watches me, sensing the shift in my demeanour; but I've already made up my mind.

"I'll wait in the car for five minutes," I declare, my voice firm and unwavering. "If you're not there, I'm going on my own."

I stride out of the room, my footsteps heavy with the weight of our situation. Each step feels like an eternity as I make my way to the car, my mind racing with thoughts of Sienna and what those bastards might be doing to her. Is she even alive?

Fuck, Marcus. What have you done?

Settling into the driver's seat, I clench the steering wheel tightly, trying to quell the storm of emotions raging inside me. I watch the clock on the dashboard change.

11:32. 11:33. 11:34. Those agonising minutes pass before the passenger door creaks open, and Dean slides into the seat beside me; his expression hardened, gun in hand. We share a tense glance, before Dean's voice breaks the silence.

"Let's kill some people." he says, his words finally laced with a fierce resolve.

I meet Dean's gaze with a surge of adrenaline coursing through me, and a genuinely proud smile spreads across my face.

"That's more fucking like it."

As we reach the warehouse once again, I can feel the tension thickening in the air. Dean's plan to wait outside this time feels like the right call, a contrast to my reckless charge in last night. We slip into a hidden parking spot, obscured from view but offering a perfect vantage point to survey the warehouse entrance.

The minutes tick by like grains of sand in an hourglass, each one an excruciating reminder of the waiting game we're forced to play. Hours dissolve into an endless expanse of silence, punctuated only by the occasional flicker of a passing car or the distant hum of machinery. Every second feels like an eternity, each tick of the clock a slow, agonizing torture as we remain fixed, our eyes riveted on the building before us.

But finally, our patience pays off. A buff figure emerges and heads towards the warehouse entrance. My heart jumps into my throat as I recognize him. It's Moth.

Dean and I share a knowing look. This is it, our chance to fight back and bring Sienna home.

With a silent agreement, we slip out of the car and move stealthily towards the warehouse, our senses sharp and our movements calculated. We reach the door, and as Dean and I meet each other's gaze, the past unfurls before us like a tapestry. The countless moments of laughter, of danger, of sacrifice; all the memories we've shared flash through our minds in a single, electric moment. It's as if we're speaking a language that transcends words, our eyes conveying a depth of understanding and connection that can only be forged through shared experiences. And now, facing this together, guns in hand, our bond feels stronger than ever.

We know what needs to be done, and we're in this together.

With that, I boot the door open; our hearts beating as one. As we storm into the warehouse, Moth stands there, examining the wreckage of the cars. His eyes blaze with fury as he takes in the sight of us, both armed. I waste no time, my voice dripping with disdain as I taunt him.

"Sorry about the cars, mate." Moth's face twists into an immediate mask of rage, his fists clenched at his sides.

"You will be, you little shits." Moth sneers, his voice dripping with venom. "Come back for more, have ya?" My grip tightens on my gun, my jaw set in determination.

"Absolutely." Moth's lips curl into a smirk, his eyes glinting with malice.

"Why are you doing all the talking, ay?" he taunts. "You're not exactly our top priority here. The Boss wants the blondie." he nods towards Dean.

"I don't give a fuck about any of that," I start as I stride closer, my eyes locked onto my target, "Where's Sienna?" Moth's laughter cuts through the tension, purposefully loud and mocking.

"Ahh, Sienna," he taunts, his voice dripping with derision. "What do you care? She's nothing to you now. In fact, she's been quite entertaining while you've been busy with your little heroics."

My jaw clenches with fury.

"What the fuck are you talking about?" I growl, my voice barely contained. Moth's smirk widens into a cruel teeth-baring grin as he continues to provoke me.

"You know exactly what I'm talking about," he jeers, his tone filled with malicious glee. "Let's just say, our little Sienna's been keeping us quite satisfied in your absence."

Oh yeah, he's about to fucking die.

My vision blurs with rage, the urge to lash out nearly overwhelming. But I reign in my anger until I can find out exactly where they're holding her.

"You have no idea the things we did to her, brother." he sneers, relishing in his adversary's torment. "We showed her a whole new world." I stride forward until we're face to face, my gun held firmly into his side.

"Tell me where she is." I repeat, my voice edged with a lethal threat.

"Drop the gun and I might, pretty boy."

For a tense moment, nobody moves, the air thick with anticipation. Then, with a reluctant nod, I release my grip on the weapon, allowing it to clatter to the ground. Fuck the gun. Once I know where my sweet is, I'll kill this cunt regardless.

"Where is she?" I state, my patience wearing thin. But instead of answering, the prick's grin widens, a dark glint in his eyes.

"Oh, man," he purrs, his voice laced with cruelty. "She felt so fucking good."

With each vile utterance that drips from his lips, my rage ignites like a wildfire, quickly burning away all reason and restraint. My muscles tense with the effort to contain the torrent of emotions coursing through me; my jaw clenched so tight it feels as if it might shatter. He dares to speak again, each word laced with sadistic pleasure.

"Oh brother, you have no idea the pain we put her through. The way her body trembled as we took her, one by one. *Corr.* We passed her around like a fuckin' blunt."

I never truly understood the concept of 'seeing red'.
Until now.
Now I understand.

I'm seeing fucking red. Drowning in it. Every breath tastes like his blood. As I'm staring into his eyes, he's not a man standing before me. He's a walking corpse, a soul already damned. I can smell the stench of death radiating from him. He takes another step closer to me.

"From the moment she stepped foot into our hellhole, we made damn sure she knew who was in charge. We toyed with her head 'till she didn't know which way was up, just so we could watch the hope drain from her eyes when she realised she was fucked."

"I won't fucking ask you again. Where. Is. She?"

No answer.

"We pinned her down like animals, held her helpless beneath us as we ravaged her little body in ways you can't even begin to imagine. Left her raw and bleeding. We made her beg, made her scream for mercy, knowing damn well we weren't gonna give her none. And she screamed, *God*, did she scream."

Fuck red. I'm seeing black. I'm seeing him in a bloodbath so gruesome, it'll make your stomach churn.

"You wanna know the worst part? She screamed out for *you*, brother. Cried out for you to come and save her. And where were you, ay?"

I charge at him, my fists swinging like hammers. I can feel the satisfying crunch of bone beneath my knuckles, the sickening squelch of flesh. Every blow is a release, a cathartic purge of all the anger and frustration that's been building inside me since they took her. I want to see him suffer.

Moth's cries of pain are drowned out by the sounds of my blood pumping in my ears and the echoes of Sienna's screams in my mind, a symphony of vengeance unleashed upon the vile creature before me. Blood sprays across my face, hot and sticky against my skin. I taste it on my lips, fuelling my rage; driving me to new heights of brutality.

Moth lies battered on the ground before me, but I'm not done. I grab him by the collar, pulling him up so I can look him in the eyes. I want him to see the fury burning within me, to know that he brought this upon himself. He's about to pay for his sins in blood.

"I'm gonna ask you one more fucking time. Where is she?"

"Okay, okay, fuck! I'll tell you." he stammers, his voice trembling with pain.

"Now!" His eyes dart around the room before they land on a workbench at the back.

"She's in a house just a few streets up," he blurts out, desperation evident in his voice. "The address is written on a piece of paper over there."

I narrow my eyes, studying Moth's expression for any signs of deception. But there's no denying the raw terror in his eyes, the desperation of a man who knows he's on the brink of his own demise. I turn to Dean.

"Check it," I bark, my voice sharp and commanding. "Make sure he's not lying." Dean nods, his jaw set with determination as he strolls leisurely towards the workbench. Meanwhile, I fix my focus on Moth, my eyes boring into his.

"I'm telling the truth, brother. C'mon.." I don't respond, instead choosing to remain a steady gaze on the vermin in my hand.

Finally, Dean makes his way back over, standing in front of me, a triumphant grin plastered across his face.

"He's telling the truth," he announces, holding up a piece of paper with an address scrawled on it.

"See, I told ya." he has the audacity to murmur.

"I'm glad." I start, "but unfortunately for you, it doesn't matter."

"Please, man!" he pleads *oh-so* satisfyingly.

"And you wanna know the worst part?"

"I apologise, man! C'mon!"

"We just toyed with your head until you didn't know which way was up, just so we could watch the hope drain from your eyes when you realise that you're fucked."

I don't hesitate. With a swift motion, I draw my knife, the blade's deadly edge glinting with an ominous light in the dimly lit room. Without a shred of pity or mercy, I press the razor-sharp edge against Moth's throat, savouring the stark terror that wells up in his eyes like a dark, icy pool.

"This is for Sienna."

With deliberate slowness, I begin to draw the blade across Moth's throat, savouring every agonised whimper that escapes his lips. The crimson torrent erupts, painting his clothes and the floor with a macabre canvas of crimson, as his life force bleeds out in a slow, agonising trickle. I carve him like a fucking pumpkin.

Moth thrashes and struggles, but I hold him firm, my grip unyielding as I continue to slice deeper and deeper. Dean aids me, stepping firmly on his forehead to keep him steady. The metallic tang of blood fills the air.

But I don't stop there. No, I keep going, driven by a primal urge for vengeance that consumes me from within. I stab, and I stab, and I stab. With each stab of the knife, I feel the weight of my torment and anger lifting from my shoulders, replaced by a savage satisfaction that's almost intoxicating. I stab until every feature on his face blurs into one mushy pile of flesh and bone.

Moth's head hangs from his neck, almost as if it's barely tethered to his body. Hanging by threads. The muscles inside his neck twitch chaotically, giving me goosebumps as I watch the life drain from his eyes. There's a sickening gurgle as blood continues to spurt from the gaping wound in his throat, the crimson liquid pooling on the floor beneath him in a gushing puddle.

Despite the horror unfolding before me, I feel good. Really, really fucking good. So good you wouldn't believe.

Finally, with one last gurgling gasp, Moth falls silent, his lifeblood spilling out onto the floor in a gruesome tableau of death. I watch impassively as the light fades from his eyes, knowing that *some* justice has been served.

As I finally stand up, my muscles still trembling with the remnants of adrenaline, I look down on Moth's lifeless body. With a mixture of satisfaction and disgust, I raise my foot and deliver a hard kick to his side, the impact eliciting a dull thud; before spitting on his motionless form.

But before I can turn away, Dean steps forward, a glint of malice in his eyes.

"And just for good luck," he says, his voice dripping with contempt.

Without hesitation, he raises his weapon and unleashes a barrage of bullets into Moth's already mangled head. The sound of gunfire reverberating through the room, each shot a final punctuation mark on the gruesome scene before us.

As the echoes of the shots fade away, I feel a sense of closure wash over me. Moth may have been an architect of torment, but now he's nothing more than a bloody corpse, his reign of terror extinguished for good.

"Let's go get my girl."

CHAPTER 24:
CHARLOTTE

Sienna

I sit on the edge of the bed, my mind swirling with a mix of boredom and desperation. The silence in the room is suffocating, weighing heavy on my chest like a leaden blanket. It must've been hours since Noah left me here, alone and isolated, with nothing but my thoughts for company; drifting into unsettling territory.

I've started to notice the little things, the subtle changes in my surroundings. I find myself watching my own bruises, tracing the patterns with my fingertips and studying them with a morbid fascination. I wonder if they'll change, if they'll somehow fade away as I stare. I listen to the sound of my own heartbeat, the steady rhythm echoing in the silence like a drumbeat of despair. Each thud is a reminder that I am still alive.

My eyes glue to the darkened stains that mar the floor and soak into the bedding.

Is this where I'm going to die?

I used to think that the way my parents went was a horrible way to die, to be snatched away so suddenly, with no warning. But now, as I sit here in this dark, forsaken place, I can't help but wonder if their fate was a mercy compared to mine. I'm certain that looking down on me in this room, they would be praying for me to meet death the way they did. It'd be a privilege.

At least they were spared the agony of knowing what was coming, the slow, agonising descent into darkness. At least they were spared the torment of being violated, of having their bodies defiled by those who would seek to break them.

Suddenly the door bursts open, flooding the room with blinding light that leaves me disoriented and blinking furiously. For a moment, I can't make sense of what I'm seeing, my mind struggling to process the sudden intrusion. But as my eyes adjust to the harsh glare, the scene before me comes into focus with chilling clarity. My heart lurches in my chest as one of the men barges in, tossing a woman onto the floor with a cruel disregard, before locking the door once again. The sound of her body hitting the ground echoes in the silence.

I sit in shock, as I watch her crumple to the ground in a heap. She's naked, just like me, her body covered in bruises and cuts that mirror my own. I'm frozen, unable to tear my eyes away from her broken form. Fear and shock grip me like icy tendrils, rendering me speechless and immobile.

Every fibre of my being screams at me to do something, to reach out and offer comfort to this stranger who shares my torment. But I'm paralyzed, trapped in a suffocating bubble of terror that squeezes the breath from my lungs.

And then, almost imperceptibly, she tilts her head upward, and our eyes meet fully for the first time.

It's as if the darkness itself has come to life, two piercing orbs locking onto mine with an unblinking intensity that sears my soul. I find myself unable to tear my eyes away from hers. I feel a lump form in my throat as I struggle to find my voice.

"Hello," I manage to whisper, my voice barely audible above the pounding of my heart.

"Hello?" she murmurs, clearly in shock.

"Hi." It feels strange to speak, as if the sound of my own voice is foreign to me.

"How long have you been here?" she asks, her tone filled with disbelief.

"I.. I'm not sure," I stammer, taken aback by the intensity of her gaze. "I think about a day." Her confusion seems palpable as she fires off questions.

"What's your name?" she asks, her voice trembling with a mixture of fear and uncertainty.

"Sienna," I reply, as I struggle to make sense of the situation. "What's *your* name?"

"Charlotte." she snaps out, "Why are you here?" she demands, her voice growing more urgent with each passing moment.

"I don't know," I admit, my voice choked with emotion. Her brow furrows in confusion.

"But you must know something," she insists, her voice rising with frustration as she moves closer to me. "You must remember something about how you ended up here. You.. you must have some idea. This room is empty, it's always empty." Her words are flustered and frantic and I'm struggling to keep up.

"Then what is this room for?" She seems to be frustrated everytime I ask her a question, as though she's running out of time.

"I get thrown in here for a few minutes every now and then while they 'clean' the room next door."

she tells me in a rush, "The man who just threw me in, did he bring you here?"

I close my eyes, trying to block out the flood of memories that threaten to overwhelm me. I nod my head quickly.

"Yes, and three others."

"*Four* men brought you here? Are you sure? I've only ever met three men here aside from Grizzly." she stammers disorderly and in complete and utter disbelief. I nod, my eyes widening with confusion and a sliver of fear.

"I'm sure."

"Four men?" she mumbles to herself, "I don't mean to pry, it's just.." she continues, her voice growing more frantic with each word, "I must've been down here for almost 20 years now and.. and there's never been anybody else brought here."

Charlotte's words hit me like a ton of bricks.

Twenty years?

The realisation sinks in slowly, seeping into the recesses of my mind like a spreading stain. I feel a cold sweat break out across my skin. The thought of spending the next two decades trapped in this hellish prison fills me with a bone-deep dread. Twenty years of torment, rape, loneliness. Twenty years of pain and suffering. Twenty years of endless nights spent lying awake, counting the minutes until morning comes and the cycle begins anew.

"We have to get out of here." I declare, my voice trembling with newfound determination. Charlotte's eyes widen with alarm, her lips parting in disbelief.

"Oh, honey," she murmurs, her voice thick with emotion As she places a quick, comforting hand on mine. "There's no getting out." Her words hit me like a physical blow. For a moment, I'm speechless, her blunt answer crashing down on me with brutal force.

"No," I finally whisper, shaking my head in denial. "There has to be a way. If we work together!" A surge of anger rises within me, hot and fierce, burning away the numbness that has enveloped me like a shroud.

I can't just sit here and accept this fate. Not after what happened last night. Not after the way they violated me, their hands rough and cruel as they roamed my body. The tiny glimpse I've had of this life is enough for me. I refuse to let that be my reality.

"We have to fight back." I spit out the words, my voice cracking. Charlotte's eyes stretch wide in shock, her fingers digging into my hand as if she's desperate to anchor herself to me.

"Don't be ridiculous," she scoffs, her voice tinged with resignation. "Look at me, Sienna. I'm skin and bones. How do you expect me to fight back? You fight at all and you'll be punished for it."

The door explodes open, slamming shut behind the pair of men who storm in, their faces illuminated by the harsh light. The skinny man who had brought Charlotte in earlier returns alongside the bearded man I also met yesterday, their faces twisted into scowls of anger.

"Hey! We didn't put you in here so you bitches could chit chat." one of them barks, his voice thick with menace. Their eyes lock on Charlotte and I, sitting together on the bed, and their expressions darken with fury. It's clear that they're not pleased to find us conversing.

Without a word, the bearded man strides forward, his hand darting out like a snake to snatch Charlotte up by the arm. She cries out in pain as he yanks her roughly to her feet, his grip like a vice around her slender wrist.

In a moment of blind rage and desperation, I find myself rising to my feet, my body moving on instinct alone.

"Get off of her!" I shout, my voice cracking with emotion as I reach out to grab the man's arm. Before I can even register what I'm doing, I sink my teeth into his flesh, biting down hard with all the force I can muster. He recoils with a yelp of pain, his grip on Charlotte loosening just enough for her to break free. As I sink my teeth into the man's arm, a surge of pain shoots through my own body as his free hand lashes out, punching me with a force that sends me sprawling to the ground. The impact jolts me, knocking the breath from my lungs as I land with a sickening thud.

Stars dance before my eyes as I struggle to push myself back up, my head spinning with dizziness. Through the haze of pain, I can hear Charlotte's cries growing louder, mingling with the shouts of the men as they punish her for my actions. Trembling with a mixture of fear and anger, I force myself to my feet, my muscles screaming in protest. Blood drips from the corner of my mouth, but I ignore the pain, my focus fixed solely on Charlotte.

But as I stagger forward, my legs feeling like lead weights beneath me, I realise with a sinking feeling that it's too late. The other man has already seized her, his grip like iron as he drags her back into the room next door.

As the men loom over me, their eyes gleaming with malice, I steel myself for the onslaught to come. But nothing could prepare me for the violation that follows.

"So you wanna bite, huh?" He yells. "You think you're fucking tough?"

"Clearly she didn't learn her fucking lesson." Their hands roam my body, groping and grabbing with a sickening sense of entitlement. I recoil in horror, my skin crawling with revulsion as his touch sears into my flesh like a branding iron.

One of them pins me down on my back, his weight crushing me as he presses against me; restraining my arms above my head. I struggle beneath him, but he only laughs, his grip unyielding. His breath is hot against my skin, his foul words like a poison in my ears.

Meanwhile, the other man circles around me, a sick grin on his face. He spits on his fingers before forcing my legs apart, his intentions clear. Time seems to slow to a crawl as I watch in horror, every movement drawn out in agonising detail. His fingers inch closer to my most intimate parts, a slow-motion nightmare unfolding before my eyes.

The world narrows down to a singular focus: the impending violation, the violation I cannot allow to happen.

'Then fight, sweet.'

With a surge of adrenaline, I summon every last ounce of strength and drive my knee into his tiny little balls with all the force I can muster. He doubles over with a grunt of pain, causing the other man's hold on me to loosen momentarily. Seizing the opportunity, I break free and scramble to my feet, my heart pounding in my chest as I make a desperate bid for freedom.

'Show me what you've got.'

With every ounce of strength I possess, I fight back, lashing out with all the fury of a cornered animal. I claw at their faces, rake my nails down their arms, bite, hit, kick, anything to make it stop.

The fight rages on but despite my best efforts, I'm outnumbered, outmatched, and outgunned. Their fists rain down on me with merciless force, each strike sending shockwaves of pain rippling through my battered body.

"Come on little girl. Just give up and get it over with." the bearded man laughs. I grit my teeth, my fists flying in a desperate bid to fend them off.

"Fuck you!" I shout, my voice raw with defiance.

But it's like trying to hold back a tidal wave with my bare hands. I can't win.

With a final, brutal blow, I'm sent crashing to the ground, the impact jolting the breath from my lungs. I lie there, gasping for air, as they descend upon me like vultures, their hands tearing at my skin, their vile laughter ringing in my ears. Their fingers ram inside me as I scream out in rage and the most intense frustration I've ever experienced.

"That's better." one of them taunts, his voice a sickening whisper in my ear. "Pathetic bitch." Before I can react, he slices through my thighs again, leaving behind a searing trail of pain. I bite back a scream, my body convulsing with agony.

But even as I lie there, bleeding, I refuse to give them the satisfaction of seeing me cry. I grit my teeth, fighting back the tears, as they walk away.

They turn to close the door, leaving me alone in the suffocating darkness of the room, when I catch sight of their bleeding arms and a deep scratch on one of their faces.

As the door slams shut behind them, the room descends once more into suffocating blackness. But I'm not sad. Believe it or not, I feel powerful. The satisfaction that surges through me is electric. A feral grin creeping onto my face, raw and untamed.

I drew blood.

CHAPTER 25:
GET READY

Dean

As we step out of the warehouse, the chill of the air hits me like a slap in the face, jolting me back to reality. My mind is a whirlwind of chaos, trying to process everything that just happened. It's like a bad dream that I can't shake off. I glance over at Marcus, his expression stoic as ever.. somehow.

Don't get me wrong, I've seen and done a lot of shit. Foul, violent, evil shit. But nothing like what just went on in that warehouse. The casual taunts of Sienna's abuse, the blood, the bones, the hanging-off head. It's too graphic to comprehend. Marcus seems to be desensitised. But me? I'm shaken up.

Just as I'm about to join Marcus in the car, my phone rings. It's Delilah. I answer quickly, trying to keep the tremor out of my voice.

"Yo, baby." I say, my voice sounding hollow and distant even to my own ears.

"Dean, where are you? I've been calling all morning." she says, her voice filled with concern.

"I'm sorry I've just been.. Uh-" I reply, struggling to find the right words as my mouth begins watering with nausea. "We've been working on some stuff."

There's a pause on the other end of the line, and I can feel Delilah's worry through the phone.

"Are you okay?" she asks softly, her voice tinged with anxiety. I take a deep breath, feeling a rush of gratitude for Delilah's presence and care. Just the sound of her voice makes me feel calmer.

"Honestly baby, it's been a rough couple days." I admit, my voice cracking with emotion. "Sienna was taken from her room and we've been trying to track her down." There's a long silence before Delilah speaks again.

"Oh dear God, is she okay?"

"We don't know. Marcus just uh.. Just killed one of the guys who grabbed her and we're heading to the address he gave us now. I'm so sorry baby but I have to go."

I can hear my darling Delilah holding her tears back through the phone.

"Please, please be safe, okay?"

"Always. I love you." I reply, feeling a lump form in my throat.

With that, I hang up the phone and slide into the driver's seat, the leather cool against my skin. As Marcus sits calmly in the passenger seat beside me, I start the engine.

"You good?" he asks, his voice low and measured. I force a tight smile and nod.

"Yeah, bro, I'm fine. I'm glad you did that." I grip the steering wheel tightly. I'm not fine, not even close. But I can't let Marcus see that. Can't let him see the cracks in my facade.

"Me too."

"Are you ready to see her? You know, after what he told us." Marcus studies me for a moment, but quickly shrugs and looks away.

"I don't even know if what he said was true, man. I just need to bring her home."

As we near the house, tension coils in my chest like a spring, every nerve on high alert. Marcus's glare sweeps the surroundings, his face a mask of concentration. I'm drawn to the imposing edifice looming before us, its massive walls rising like a monolith from the earth. It's a large home, surrounded by a high black gate that looms like a fortress wall.

Several sleek cars are parked in the driveway, their polished surfaces glinting.

The house itself is grand and imposing, exuding an aura of wealth and privilege, a stark contrast to the darkness that we know lurks within. Marcus' jaw is clenched tight, his eyes fixed on the house with laser-like focus. I can tell he's assessing the situation, weighing our options with precision. I swallow hard, trying to quell the rising sense of unease in my gut.

Sienna could be right there, trapped behind those imposing walls, and time is running out.

But then, just as we're about to pull up to the curb, three men emerge from the house. My heart leaps into my throat, and I instinctively slam on the brakes, swerving sharply to the side and ducking out of sight. The car jerks to a halt, the engine still running as we sit in silence, hidden from their view.

I steal a glance at Marcus, his features tight with tension. His eyes are fixed on the men outside, tracking their movements with hawk-like precision. We hold our breath, the seconds stretching into eternity as the men drive off. Only when they're out of sight do we release the breath we've been holding, a collective sigh of relief. My hands tremble slightly as I wipe the sweat from my brow.

"Holy fuck." I mutter.

"Three less cunts to worry about, right?" I nod with a slight chuckle, my own pulse still racing from the close call.

"But how many more inside?"

Marcus' expression darkens at the reminder, his jaw clenched tight with determination. I can see the gears turning in his mind as he calculates our next move, weighing the risks.

"I can't wait any longer," he says, his voice low and urgent. "Let's fucking go." I nod in agreement, a surge of adrenaline coursing through my veins at the prospect of finally confronting the monsters who took Sienna from us. It's time to bring her home.

CHAPTER 26:
SAVING SWEET SIENNA

Sienna

I can't get Charlotte off of my mind.

I can't unsee her.

I can't unhear her.

Her presence lingers in this room like a ghost.

Minutes are blending into hours.

Hours are feeling like days.

The pain is a constant companion. It's no longer a sensation; it's a living, breathing entity that coils around my limbs, gnawing at my flesh. Every movement is agony, a symphony of torment that plays out in every fibre of my being.

I can't escape it. It's everywhere.

Like a suffocating shroud that clings to me, refusing to let go. I run my hands over my body, searching for any patch of unharmed skin, but there's none to be found. Bruises bloom like grotesque flowers across my flesh, their colours shifting from sickly purples to angry reds.

I've learned to navigate the pain, in a twisted sort of way. I have discovered that hurting one part of my body can distract from the unrelenting pain of another.

A sharp pinch to my arm momentarily dulls the ache in my side. A hard stub of my toe removes the pain from my temples.

But it's still a cycle.

I think over Charlotte's words. Twenty years. I can't fathom it. The prospect of spending the next twenty years locked away in this bleak, soul-sucking hellhole fills me with a creeping bone-deep dread. How could I possibly survive another day, let alone twenty years? I can lie to myself all I want. Pretend all I want. The truth is, I'm not strong enough. I'm not strong enough to endure twenty years of this relentless torture, to face each day with the knowledge that there may never be an escape. The thought alone terrifies me.

How is it possible that I've met more people in a single day than Charlotte has in twenty years? *Aside from 'Grizzly' of course.* I'm yet to have that encounter.

And they were together. She was fucking dating the guy! The thought is incomprehensible. This whole thing is like trying to fit a square peg into a round hole. How did she get herself tangled up with someone so fucked up he would lock her in a basement for twenty years?

Says the girl happily in love with a murderer.

But then a tiny voice in the back of my mind whispers some truth; maybe it does make some twisted sort of sense. They knew each other, they had some kind of history. At least there's a thread, no matter how thin.. right?
But what about Dean? Me?

I lie down on the rough, hard bed, the bare mattress biting into my skin like a thousand tiny needles. I close my eyes, hoping that sleep will eventually come. But it doesn't.

I never realised just how many noises the human body makes.

In the dead silence I become acutely aware of the sound of my own breath, a rasping wheeze that fills the air with each inhalation and exhalation. The sound of my own blood pumping around my body. The gurgles in my stomach.

Although, those sounds are tolerable. They're Understandable. Expected.

It's the stranger noises that keep me awake.

There's the soft click of my eyelids closing, the flutter of my eyelashes on my skin. There's the unsettling squelch of my organs shifting inside me, the wet, slurping noise that seems to echo in the hollow cavity of my chest; the creak of my joints as I switch position. There's the soft, wet sound of my tongue clicking against the roof of my mouth, the rustle of an endless stream of saliva that I keep needing to swallow.

But it's not just the sounds of my internal organs that distract me. There are other, more disturbing noises; the strange clicking and popping sounds that seem to come from within my own head.

A squelching sound emanating from between my legs. A perverse echo reverberating off the walls and crawling beneath my skin.

Then, a sudden break in the monotony; a faint flicker of light seeps through the bottom of the door, casting a feeble glow into the darkness. My heart lurches at the sight, my mind racing with possibilities. Not yet has this particular light shone through.

As a soft shuffle of footsteps descends the staircase, every nerve in my body is on edge. Each creak of wood reverberates through the silence like a gunshot. They're coming back. Panic sets in, and I scramble to hide beneath the bed.

But then the muffle of a voice breaks through.
It sounds like Marcus, my mind whispers.

It's a cruel lie. My hopeful brain playing tricks on me. I'm beginning to hallucinate.

Yet, the voice persists, growing louder and more insistent with each passing moment.

"Bro, check this out," it says.

Holy fuck. It *is* him.

Without a second thought, I launch myself towards the door, my heart pounding like a jackhammer in my chest. Every muscle in my body screams with exertion as I sprint across the room, my feet pounding against the cold, hard floor. I feel like I'm flying. Panic and desperation drive me forward, fueling my pained movements as I reach the door and unleash a barrage of fists upon its splintered surface.

"Marcus!" I scream, my voice raw with emotion. "Marcus, I'm here!"

Tears blur my vision as I pound on the door with all my strength, each blow reverberating through the room like a thunderclap.

"Sienna?!" he shouts back, his footsteps quickly descending closer.

With every passing second, the walls behind me feel like they're closing in, the space around me shrinking; as if the darkness itself is chasing me down. But I refuse to be swallowed by the void.

With every ounce of strength I possess, I continue to hammer away at the door, my cries growing louder and more frantic with each passing second.

"I'm in here, Marcus! Please!"

MARCUS

I cannot fucking breathe.

Sienna's piercing screams and cries are breaking right through me.
I've never heard a scream like that before.

My heart thumps like a drum on steroids, pounding out a rhythm of stress and desperation as I fuck up almost every single lock first time, my fingers shaking so hard I can barely get a grip. With each clunk of metal, my chest tightens like a vice.

Each tortured cry is a stab to my heart, a reminder of the nightmare she's living while I stand here fumbling with the disgusting amount of locks on this fucking door.

With a final, desperate twist, the last lock gives way, and the door flies open, flooding the dark room holding her with a blinding light.

As I take in the sight of Sienna, my heart constricts with a visceral agony.
Nothing, absolutely nothing, could've prepared me for what I see before me.

She's a shadow of my sweet. Beaten, battered, bleeding, dirty.. Naked. Her body a canvas of cuts and bruises. Every tear in her flesh is a searing indictment of my failure to protect her. Dark thoughts swarm through my mind like a plague of locusts, each one more sinister than the last. As I take in every mark on her body I imagine how it came to be.

How could I have let this happen?

Without hesitation, I launch myself at her, my arms wrapping around her trembling little body. I hold her as tight as I possibly can, trying to shield her from the horrors that surround us; as if by sheer force of will I can erase the pain and anguish etched into every line of her battered face. Her sobs and guttural screams echo in my ears.

"*Oh God*, sweet." I whisper to her, my voice entirely shaky. "I'm so sorry."

Tears blur my vision as I press my lips to her forehead, murmuring words of comfort and solace against her skin.

"I'm here, okay? I'm here, I've got you. Nobody's gonna hurt you, sweet. I promise." I don't know if she can hear me, if she can even comprehend.

I've failed her.

As I cradle her in my arms, her sobs reverberating against my chest, I cast my gaze around the room. Bloodstains mar the cold, hard floor.

My eyes catch on to the only piece of furniture in the room. A metal double bed, its frame devoid of any bedding save for a bare mattress. It looms in the dim light like a sacrificial altar, a grotesque symbol of the sickening depths of moral turpitude to which humanity can sink.

As I stare at the bed, Moth's words spiral around my mind.

'We pinned her down like animals, held her helpless beneath us as we ravaged her little body in ways you can't even begin to imagine.'

Believe me, I'm doing far more than imagining it.
I can see it.
I can see her on that bed.

'We made her beg, made her scream for mercy, knowing damn well we weren't gonna give her none. And she screamed, God, did she scream.'

The agonising screams coming from her right now are confirmation.
The cunt wasn't lying.
'You wanna know the worst part? She screamed out for you, brother. Cried out for you to come and save her. And where were you, ay?'

He wasn't. Fucking. Lying.

I promised that I would protect her.
Told her she was safe with me.
Earned her trust.
And then I put her here.

I put her on that fucking bed.

My hands tremble as I hold her close, feeling her shivering against me, her frail form seeming so small and fragile in my arms. She feels smaller than usual. More fragile.

"I'm sorry, sweet. I'm so sorry."
But apologies are meaningless now, mere whispers.

As Sienna slowly pulls away from the embrace, her tear-streaked face turns up to meet mine. Her eyes, once vibrant and full of life, now seem dull and haunted.

"You came." she whimpers. Her words are like a knife to the heart. Tears well up in my eyes as I nod, unable to find the words to express the overwhelming flood of emotions. The disbelief in her voice, the faint tremor of uncertainty, it tears me apart inside.

How could she even question whether I'd come for her? As if there was ever a choice.

All I can do is reach out and gently cup her cheek, tracing the lines of her face with trembling fingers.

"Sienna," I choke out, my voice breaking. "Of course, I came. I'd have watched the world burn around me to find you. I'd have let everything else fade to ashes. "

Dean steps into the room, his footsteps hesitant, his eyes widening in shock as they take in the scene before him. His focus flits from the bloodstains on the floor to Sienna's battered form, his breath catching in his throat at the sight.

"Jesus Christ," he murmurs, the words escaping him in a hoarse whisper. Shock and horror ripple across his features, his hands instinctively reaching out to steady himself against the doorframe.

Dean and I share a look, our eyes locking in a silent exchange that screams volumes. I see the raw emotion etched on his face, a mirror of my own turmoil, and for a moment, we're frozen in mutual disbelief at the depths of depravity we've stumbled upon. Sienna's voice breaks through the heavy silence.

"Marcus? Can we please get out of this room?"

I feel a lump form in my throat at the sound of her voice. Her plea hits me like a punch to the gut, the raw innocence in her voice tearing at my heartstrings. She's just a scared, broken girl, pleading for escape from the nightmare that's consumed her. Without hesitation, I reach out and take her hand, squeezing it and kissing it gently in reassurance. Tears sting my eyes as I reach out to her.

"Of course, beautiful.

"Thank you. I love you."

"I love you too, sweet."

CHAPTER 27:
MEETING GRIZZLY

Marcus

"Let's get you out of here, sweet." As I stand, Sienna sits before me, her body shivering with exhaustion and vulnerability. I reach out instinctively, my fingers finding hers as I lift her gently onto her feet.

My eyes trace the outline of Sienna's naked body, protectiveness washing over me. I refuse to leave her exposed, even for a moment longer. Without a second thought, I shed my hoodie, the fabric heavy with my own warmth and the weight of my determination to shield her from harm.

I step closer, my fingers trembling slightly as I pull the hoodie over her head and arms. The gesture more intimate than any words could convey. It's not just about keeping her warm; it's about giving her back a piece of the dignity and safety that's been stolen from her.

For a moment, there's just the sound of her breath catching in her throat, and then she looks up at me; Her eyes dark, filled with tears and something else I can't quite name. Gratitude, maybe. Relief. Whatever it is, it's enough to make the ache in my chest ease just a little.

As we start our ascent up the stairs, Sienna suddenly yells, catching me off guard.

"Wait!" Before I can even process her words, she releases my hand and rushes back down the stairs, her urgency palpable in every hurried little step. I watch intently, my curiosity piqued, as she reaches the bottom.

With nimble fingers, she begins to unlock the door to the room next to hers. Her fingers deftly find the sliding locks; there's a determined glint in her eye. Her actions deliberate. With one final motion the last lock clicks, echoing off the walls. As the door pops open, she pauses for a moment on the threshold, her breath catching in her throat.

When Sienna returns to us on the stairs, I don't hesitate to gather her into my arms, her body fitting perfectly against mine, as if belongs there.

Because it does.

We inch our way towards the front door, our hearts pounding. Each step feels like a victory. But that changes when we reach the front door.

It's locked.
Locked by a key that we don't have.

I turn to Sienna, trying to give her some kind of reassurance, but all I see is the same fear and confusion mirrored in her eyes. It's like a punch to the gut, the realisation sinking in that our escape might not be as simple as I made her believe.

Desperate for answers, I turn to Dean, but his gaze is fixed elsewhere, his expression pale and drawn. Following his line of sight into the living room, my stomach twists with dread. Something's not right.
And then, as if on cue, a familiar voice slices through the silence like a blade.

"Goin' somewhere?" I whirl around, my breath catching in my throat, to see a figure seated on the sofa.

My heart stops dead in my chest.
It's my dad.

My eyes lock onto the face, and my mind reels in denial as I try to reconcile the reality before me. Shock freezes me in place, a surge of disbelief coursing through my veins like ice water. My breath catches in my throat, my pulse pounding in my ears as I struggle to comprehend what I'm seeing.

"What's wrong, boy?" he asks "Look like you've seen a ghost."

This can't be happening. It can't be real. But as I meet his gaze, the hard lines etched into his face, I know with a sinking certainty that it is. As I lay eyes on my father, a surge of raw emotion courses through me; anger, resentment, and a deep-seated fear.
My father's presence in a place like this can't mean anything good.

"Dad.. what's going on?"

"I'll ask the fuckin' questions," he says, immediately raising his voice, "and it ain't dad right now, boy. You'll call me fuckin' Grizzly."

The revelation hits me like a freight train, the weight of it crashing down on me with a force I can scarcely comprehend. My dad? My fucking dad? The epitome of evil incarnate. And he's sitting right here, in front of me, as if it's the most natural thing in the world.

"I'm disappointed, Marcus," he continues, his tone now chillingly calm. "You were so fuckin' easy to lure. So pathetically predictable. I thought I raised you better than that."

A bitter laugh escapes me; a sharp, mirthless sound that cuts through the tension like a knife.

"Raised me?" I chuckle. "You didn't fucking raise me." Grizzly's lips curl into a twisted grin, his eyes gleaming with a sinister glint.

"Maybe I should've," he sneers, his voice dripping with sarcasm. "Then you would've been a bit fuckin' smarter." I square my shoulders, refusing to let his intimidation get the better of me.

"What the fuck do you want from *me*?" Dean questions, his voice stern. Grizzly's leer shifts towards Dean, his expression morphing into one of disdain.

"Oh, I don't want anythin' from *you*, mate. I just got lucky since my people 'ave already been after you for some drug business." He replies, "I wanted something from my boy after he left and needed a way to track him down. I knew if we increased the pressure, Marcus would follow you 'ere like a little fuckin' puppy."

My blood runs cold at his words, the realisation sinking in like a heavy weight in the pit of my stomach. My dad had orchestrated this entire situation, pulling the strings behind the scenes.

"Ahh, okay. So let me get this straight." I begin, my voice laced with sarcasm as I take a step closer to him. "You wanted something from me and you couldn't track me down? You needed me, so you waited for me to come home and I never did?"

The air crackles with tension as Grizzly's expression darkens, his jaw clenched with suppressed rage. We stare at each other, locked in a silent battle of wills, the weight of years of resentment and unanswered questions hanging between us.

"And how did that make you feel, dad?" I ask, my words cutting through the air. "Angry? Frustrated? Stressed?"

I hold his stare, unflinching, determined to make him understand the impact of his absence on my life. Every forgotten birthday, every unanswered call, every broken vow; all the moments he was absent from my life, all the memories we never made together. I pour them into that stare, a silent rebuke to the years he spent away from me.

The silence stretches on, thick and suffocating, as Grizzly meets my gaze with a steely resolve. His lips remain sealed.

"It's funny, because I can remember feeling that too.. Dad." The tense silence stretches on, my mind swirling with a whirlwind of emotions as I grapple with the anger and resentment that has simmered beneath the surface for so long.

"I didn't bring you 'ere to talk about this bollocks." he sneers, his tone dripping with disdain. My jaw clenches in frustration, the anger boiling within me threatening to spill over.

"Then why *did* you bring me here?" I demand, my voice trembling with barely contained fury. "Why did you put us through all of this? What the fuck do you want?"

"Where's the fuckin' book, boy?"

The room falls into an absolute stunned silence. Sienna, Dean, and I exchange incredulous glances, our confusion mirrored in each other's eyes. It's so absurd, so utterly unexpected, that for a moment, it's almost comical.

"Wait, what?" I blurt out, my mind struggling to process the sudden shift in conversation. "*Book?* What book?"

Don't get me wrong. We all know exactly what book he has to be talking about, but the revelation that my dad not only knows about the book's existence but is also demanding its whereabouts has completely thrown me off.

"Don't play dumb with me. You know what I'm talking about."

"What the fuck does that book have to do with you?" I demand, my voice rising with indignation.

"Just give me the Goddamn book!" Grizzly growls, his tone dripping with impatience and barely contained anger.

"I don't have it," I reply firmly, "And even if I did, why would I give it to you?" Grizzly's nostrils flare, his fists clenching at his sides.

"It's not up for discussion, boy. Hand it over now."

"I said I don't have it!" I snap back, my voice echoing off the walls of the room.

As Grizzly's rage boils over, his face contorts into a mask of fury, veins bulging in his forehead and neck like taut cables.

"You ungrateful little shit," he snarls, taking another step closer, the classic scent of his whiskey-breath now moving towards my face.

"You owe me!"

"I owe you nothing." I spit back.

Grizzly's fury ignites, his face contorted with rage as he stands before me. All of a sudden, the ominous click of a gun being cocked echoes in the tense silence.

My heart lurches in my chest as I feel the cold, hard steel of his gun pressing against my forehead.

CHAPTER 28:

AH FUCK

Marcus

At that moment, time seems to freeze. The world narrows down to the barrel of the gun, a metal extension of my father's wrath aimed directly at me. Disbelief, anger, and a bone-deep revulsion churn within me.

It really is my father that I'm looking at.

The man who was supposed to cherish and nurture me. The man who abandoned me. The man who walked away when I needed him the most. Even when I offered him chances to make things right, he couldn't find it in himself to do so. And now, instead of seeking redemption, he's here, pointing a gun at me.

"You're pathetic." I spit out, my bottom lip quivering with anger. "You think you can make up for all those years of neglect with a gun to my head? You really think you have any power over me after everything you've done?"

But even as I speak, there's a part of me that's screaming, begging him to stop, to be the father I always needed him to be. But it's useless. He'll never change, never admit to his mistakes, never take responsibility for the pain he's caused.

"I don't wanna have to do this, son." he says, his voice strained with a twisted kind of faux-concern. "Just tell me where the book is. We can end this right now."

"I'd rather fucking die." I reply, my voice steady somehow. "I'd rather die by your hands than give you *anything* you want from me."

As I stare into his eyes, a surge of memories flood my mind. The birthdays spent alone, the nights filled with tears, the constant ache of longing for a love that was never there. A childhood he robbed from me.

At this moment, I realise that I don't owe him anything. Not obedience, not loyalty, not even a fucking book. Because he lost the right to demand anything from me the day he walked out of my life. And so, as the gun presses harder against my skin, I meet his gaze with a steely resolve.

"Do it." I say, my voice steady despite the fear clawing at my insides. "Do it! Because getting rid of me doesn't erase what you've fucking done." I declare. "You'll never erase the scars you've left behind." Time slows to a crawl as my father's hand begins to shake around the gun, his face contorting with a mix of anger and frustration.

"Do it, you fucking pussy!" I shout, the words erupting from me with a force I didn't know I possessed.

His eyes flicker with something unreadable, and then, in a sickening twist, he turns the gun towards Sienna.

"No!" I yell, my voice raw with shock as I watch in horror. The word tears from my lips, raw with alarm and desperation, but it feels small and insignificant against the impending threat. In that split second, the world narrows down to the trajectory of the bullet, my heart pounding so loudly I can barely hear anything else. It's as if time itself has ground to a halt, each passing moment stretching out into an endless, oppressive expanse..

Miraculously, the bullet misses Sienna by mere inches as she instinctively crouches to the floor, crying out in terror; her arms covering her face in a desperate attempt to shield herself. I step to the side, deliberately positioning myself between her and Grizzly. Every fibre of my being is focused on protecting her. His hand trembles around the gun, his face contorted with rage.

"You spineless cunt." I snarl, venom dripping from every word. "That make you feel tough, huh?"

"I'll pick you off one by one until I find out where that fucking book is, believe me!"

"I already told you, we don't even have the book! Get that through your fucking head!"

Grizzly's lips curl into a twisted sneer, his features contorted   with   malice.

"You're just like your mother," he spits, "both got a smart fuckin' mouth."

"I wouldn't know." I state, my voice carrying the weight of a lifetime of absence and neglect. I can see the flicker of something in his eyes, a brief glimpse of recognition, perhaps even remorse, but it's quickly overshadowed by the usual emotion of rage.

"You don't know what it was like, boy," he growls, his grip on the gun tightening. "You don't know what I've had to do to survive!"

"That's on you. Not me, dad." I retort, my voice steady somehow. "You made your choices, and now you have to live with them."

"You think you're any better than me, boy?" he snarls, the gun shaking like a leaf in his hand. "You think you're some kinda saint 'cause you've got all these morals and principles, ay? Well, lemme tell you something, son. In this world, those don't mean shit. It's survival of the fittest, and if you're not willing to do what it takes, you'll end up dead in a ditch somewhere." I meet his gaze with a steely resolve, unflinching.

"Then put me in the ditch," I retort, my voice dripping with defiance. "Buried six feet under, I'll still be standing taller than you ever fucking could."

He fills the room with a deep laughter, a bone-chilling sound that seems to reverberate off the walls. It's a sound I've heard too many times before.

"You think you're tough, don't ya?" he sneers, a cruel smile playing at the corners of his lips. "Well, let's see how tough you are when I put a bullet in your skull."

As his laughter fills the room, a bitter taste floods my mouth, a seeping sourness, but I refuse to let it shake my resolve. Suddenly, Dean steps forward, placing himself directly in front of me, his eyes locked onto Grizzly's with an intensity that sends a chill down my spine.

"What the fuck are you doing?" I hiss, trying to push him back, but he stands firm, his stare unwavering.

"Focus on Sienna." He says, his voice low but filled with conviction.

Grizzly's laughter cuts through the tension like a knife, his eyes gleaming with malice as he watches our exchange.

"Well, ain't that touchin'," he sneers, his voice dripping with sarcasm. "What a little hero." He steps forward, his gaze and gun shifting from me to Dean, his lips curling into a twisted smile.

"Dean, move." I protest, my voice breaking with emotion. "Please."

But Dean just shakes his head, his expression resolute, as he takes a step closer to my father.

"You need to protect Sienna," he insists.

Tears prickle at the corners of my eyes as I stare at him, overwhelmed by the depth of his sacrifice. In this moment, I understand what true bravery looks like; not the reckless bravado of 'Grizzly', but the quiet, selfless courage of Dean willing to lay down his life.

Protect Sienna. Protect Dean.
My entire life summed up in four words.

Grizzly tightens his grip on the gun, his finger poised on the trigger, and I feel the world around me slow to a crawl. Then, I catch a whimper from Sienna. I glance down at her, and my heart shatters at the sight of her beautiful wide eyes filled with tears and horror, taking in the scene unfolding before her.

Without a second thought, I drop to my knees, pulling her into my arms to shield her from watching any longer.

"It's okay, sweet." I whisper, my voice trembling with emotion as I press her face against my chest. "Close your eyes. I'm here, okay? I've got you." She clings to me, her small frame shaking with fear, and I hold her close, my own heart pounding in my chest as I try to comfort her.

Sienna's cries echo in the room, her tears soaking my shirt as she holds onto me. The sobs fill my ears, tearing at my heart as I rock her gently, whispering words of comfort. I press my lips against her cheek, tasting the salt of her tears, as I will away the world to disappear. With a shudder, I close my eyes, burying my head into her hair, seeking solace in the scent of her.

And then, like a bolt from the blue, the deafening crack of a gunshot shatters the fragile bubble of our sanctuary, sending shockwaves reverberating through the room; followed by the thud of a body hitting the ground. Sienna gasps, her grip on me tightening with a vice-like intensity, as if she could hold onto me forever.

And though I can't bear to look, a sickening ball lurches in the pit of my stomach; the realisation hitting me like a physical blow,

Dean's been shot.

Sienna's cries reach a crescendo, a heartbreaking symphony of fear and despair that threatens to consume us both. I hold her even closer, if that's possible. A single thought echoes in the recesses of my mind; a name, a face, a presence so integral in my life that the mere thought of this actually happening is simply incomprehensible.

But just as I'm about to succumb to the suffocating weight of uncertainty, a sudden, shocking shout pierces the silence;

a voice so familiar, so unmistakably.. Dean.

CHAPTER 29:
DELILAH

Dean

"That's my fucking girl!" I shout. The words, raw with emotion, rip from my throat as I turn, my heart pounding; to see Delilah standing there in the hallway between the living room and the kitchen. My mind struggles to comprehend the scene before me as I take her in; the gun in her hand aimed at Grizzly, who now lies lifeless on the ground. Everything else fades away; all I see is her, my saviour, my love, my everything.

My heart swells with a mixture of awe and disbelief. Without thinking, without hesitating, I charge towards her, my legs feeling like they're made of lead and feathers at the same time. My blood thrumming in my veins. I close the distance between us in a heartbeat, and before I know it, I'm sweeping her off her feet, pulling her into a desperate, frantic embrace.

"*God*, Delilah," I growl, my voice rough with emotion, as I hold her tighter. "You are amazing."

She clasps onto me just as fiercely, her nails digging into my back, her breath coming in ragged gasps. And in this embrace, in this desperate, frantic tangle of limbs and hearts, I find everything I ever knew I needed. Home.

I glimpse briefly to Marcus and Sienna, who are slowly rising to their feet behind me. Locking eyes with Marcus, I offer him a subtle nod, a silent promise that I'm still here, still standing. His eyes, brimming with tears, meet with mine, and in that raw, unfiltered moment, it's like our souls are having a conversation; saying everything we can't put into words.

As I spin Delilah around in my arms, the rush of emotions threatens to overwhelm me. She laughs, the sound like music to my ears, as I finally place her back on her feet, holding her face tight between my hands.

"How the fuck did you get here?" I ask, my voice tinged with incredulity and relief. Delilah looks up at me, her eyes sparkling with mischief and affection.

"Well, you know that phone I gave you?" she says, her tone playful and lighthearted. "I might have kinda used it to check your location." I can't help but chuckle at her admission.

"Ah, so you're a little stalker, huh?"

"Hey, desperate times call for desperate measures," she quips, her tone playful yet sincere. I can't help but shake my head in mock disapproval, though my heart swells with affection for her, entirely unable to contain the grin spreading across my face.

"Thank you for saving me, my darling." She smiles softly, her hand coming up to cup my cheek.

"Always."

As I reluctantly pull away from Delilah, a heavy feeling settles in the pit of my stomach. Turning around, I'm met with a scene that couldn't be more different from the warmth and relief I just experienced. Marcus stands over his dead father's body, his gaze fixed steadily on the lifeless form on the ground. There's a haunting stillness. My heart aches for him, for the pain and the trauma and the confused blend of emotions he must be feeling.

The grief of losing a parent he waited so long for, the relief of being freed from a lifetime of abuse, the guilt of feeling relieved, the anger at the injustice of it all. He stands at the crossroads of conflicting emotions, grappling with the aftermath of a lifetime of abuse and the sudden, stark finality of death.

As I look at Marcus I don't ever see a grown man standing at 6 foot 5. A man covered in tattoos, old enough to have a child of his own if he wanted. I see the little boy I once knew. The boy I grew up with. The boy who, like me, dreamed of a life beyond the confines of that shitty children's shelter; a life filled with love and laughter, a life that always seemed just out of reach.

Now, all he ever wanted lies dead on the floor.

He mourns not only the physical loss of his father but the shattered illusions of what could have been. He'd always craved parental love; the warmth of a real family. Birthday parties, pets, holidays; a christmas morning with a tree and a stocking. The simple things that most people take for granted.

We never did.
It's all we ever longed for.

I always saw it in Marcus' eyes. The silent plea for something he'd never received. He'd given his dad endless chances to step up, to be the father figure he desperately needed. Yet, time and time again, his pleas fell on deaf ears, drowned out by the deafening silence of indifference or punctuated by the searing sting of betrayal.

I know that feeling all too well. It's an excrutiating punch to the gut, beginning to realise and understand that the people who are supposed to love you the most couldn't care less.

Coming to terms with that. Ignoring that. Living with that. Acting like that's okay, like *you're* okay. Pretend it doesn't eat away at you every single fucking day.

"I'm fine," you say, over and over, until the words lose their meaning, until they become a mantra, a shield against the pain. They become hollow. *"I don't care,"* you repeat, like a broken record, hoping that if you say it enough times, you might actually start to believe it. But deep down, you know the truth; it's not okay, and you're not okay.

Yet you grow and you mature and eventually it genuinely does become *almost* okay. It becomes bearable. Tolerable. Forgettable. Ignorable.

Then you realise one day *you* will be a father to somebody. *You'll* be the one to make sure a child doesn't feel the way you did. That's what drives you forwards.

And that's where it ends.

The past loses its grip on you, its relevance fading into obscurity as you focus solely on building a future. Healing.

Approaching Marcus, I grip his shoulder, feeling the tension in his muscles like coiled springs.

"I'm sorry." I offer.

Scrunching his eyebrows, he points to the blood pooling on the ground.

"See that?" he says, his voice raw with emotion. "We share that." I follow his focus, feeling a lump form in my throat. He looks back to me and meets my gaze with purpose, a haunted look in his eyes. "And *we* don't," he continues, his voice heavy with regret. I offer a faint smile and airy chuckle in return.

"Fucked up, huh?"

As Marcus and I exchange tense glances, the room is suddenly rocked by a cacophony of crashing and banging against the front door. Marcus and I exchange puzzled glances as the noise grows louder, the door now shaking with each feeble impact.

With a final, desperate strike, the door gives way, folding open in a grandiose display of splintered wood and dramatic flair. And lo and behold, through the now-gaping entrance stumbles none other than Birdie and Skylar, their entrance more reminiscent of a slapstick comedy than a break-in. Birdie clutches a comically undersized 'battering ram' -a tiny, old hammer repurposed for the occasion- while Skylar follows close behind, her expression a pathetic mix of triumph and amusement.

"She wouldn't let me pick the lock." Skylar states ridiculously blunt and casual.

"Holy shit, is that a dead guy?" Birdie blurts out. The room falls into silence as we all try not to laugh, the only sound is the collective intake of breath as we process the sheer ludicrousness of the situation. Skylar's eyes widen in realisation as she takes in the scene, her expression a mix of shock and disbelief. She nudges Birdie with her elbow before attempting to whisper,

"Oh my God, Birdie! Shh, that's his dad!"

Marcus stares at them, his expression a masterclass in incredulity, with a dash of amusement and exasperation.

"Yup, that's my dad," he deadpans, his tone laced with sarcasm as he tries to keep a stern face. Following this, as if a switch had been flipped, the tension dissolves into uproarious laughter.

As the laughter fills the room, an odd mix of catharsis and absurdity. It's a strange sound, given the grim scene before us, but it's also a release. A needed release. There's a sense of unity again. We've been through so fucking much, and somehow, we always find a way to come out on the other side.

Alive and more connected than ever before.

CHAPTER 30:
A BOMBSHELL

Marcus

As my father lies dead on the floor in front of me, I feel everything all at once. Anger mostly. Lots of deep-rooted, passionate anger. He's taken the easy way out. Death has absolved him of all responsibility, leaving me to grapple with the wreckage he left behind. The fact that he's gone now feels like the ultimate betrayal, the final abandonment in a lifetime filled with them.

But he doesn't deserve my rage. I've wasted enough energy on him, and he's not worth another second of my life. I refuse to let his death define me as much as his life did.

Instead, I turn my thoughts and energy towards Sienna. My sweet Sienna, my future. She represents everything my father never was; loving, supportive, hopeful. Present. She is the light that guides me. Her body is a mosaic of bruises and cuts, her eyes haunted yet resilient.

For a moment, we just stand there.

I take a tentative step towards her, my heart aching at the sight of her pain.

"How you holding up, sweet?" I whisper, my voice cracking. She looks up at me, tears streaming down her face.

"I didn't think I'd ever get out of there, Marcus." She trembles, "I didn't think I'd ever see you again."

"I'm so sorry, sweet." I say, "I should've protected you." Sienna lifts her head, her eyes locking with mine.

"This wasn't your fault."

"But it was." I confirm, guilt gnawing at my insides. "It was all my fault. I'm supposed to keep you safe."

"You can't carry that weight, Marcus." She insists, her eyes pleading with me to see reason. "All I wanted was to see you walk through that door, and that's exactly what you did. You saved me."

You might look at somebody like me and pity the life I've been given. You might think I'm a failure. You might even feel sorry for me.

But as I look down at her right now, my entire world in my hands; those big, beautiful honey-brown eyes staring back at me, I know I'm in fact the luckiest man alive.

I pull her into a hug, laying her head against my chest. I can feel the tremors coursing through her body, matching the erratic beat of my own heart.

"I love you, Marcus." she breathes against my chest. I hold her even tighter, if that's even possible.

"I love you too, sweet." I reply, my voice thick with emotion. "More than anything." And then, as if on cue, we both break into a bittersweet smile, the weight of the world momentarily lifted from our shoulders. I squeeze and I squeeze her tighter, rocking her in a silent rhythm that speaks volumes without the need for words. Planting tender kisses upon her cheeks, I shower her with affection, each touch a testament to the depth of my adoration.

We reluctantly untangle ourselves, but our eyes stay locked. I squat down to her level, a grin spreading across my face as I take her hand in mine, pressing a kiss on her knuckles. We smile at each other. We just smile. Stare and smile. It's one of those rare moments where everything else fades away, leaving only the two of us in our own little bubble.

"You know, sweet. There is one brightside to this whole thing." I start, a hint of arrogance laced with affection in my voice.

"Do tell." she replies in a feminine tone.

"Maybe this will teach you to follow my orders in future." I smirk.

As we stand there, lost in our shared moment, a sudden interruption breaks the spell. An unfamiliar female voice echoes from behind me, jolting me out of my reverie.

"Sweet?"

As I Turn my head slowly, I'm met by a small, battered woman standing at the top of the basement stairs, wearing only a bed sheet wrapped around her. Her form is hunched, her frame fragile and worn, like a delicate porcelain doll weathered by time and circumstance.

My heart drops like a stone in my chest, a heavy weight that threatens to crush me beneath its burden. A thunderous drumbeat echoes in my ears, drowning out the sounds of the world around me. A cold sweat breaks out on my forehead as I lay eyes on the figure standing in front of me.

In an instant, the world tilts on its axis, spinning wildly out of control as the pieces of the puzzle fall into place.

The photograph from my childhood that I had tucked away in the back of the pile, in the back of my mind, races to the forefront. In a millisecond, I analyse every feature of her, a game of spot the difference playing out in my head. But there are no differences to be found, no discrepancies to reconcile.

Recognition crashes over me like a tidal wave, leaving me breathless and dizzy.
It can't be... But it is.

"Mum?"

The woman whose face has haunted my dreams, whose absence has left an ache in my heart that I couldn't name until this moment. She stands before me, a living, breathing enigma, and I'm frozen in place, unable to tear my gaze away from her.
"Yes, sweet. Yes, it's Mum!" she confirms, her voice trembling with emotion as she nods eagerly, tears streaming from her eyes.

My mind reels, struggling to process the enormity of what I'm living through. Mum? Just saying it felt so unnatural. The word echoes in my head. A distant echo, foreign and yet achingly familiar all at once.

Without hesitation, she speeds towards me, her movements desperate and urgent. As she rushes towards me, her movements fueled by a desperation I can't begin to fathom, I'm rooted to the spot, unable to move, unable to speak.

I barely have time to react before she falls into my arms, her body trembling with the weight of years of longing and separation. In that moment, time stands still, suspended in the delicate balance between what was and what could have been.

"Oh God!" She sobs.

I struggle to make sense of it all. This woman, her scent, her touch; it's all so overwhelming, so disorienting. My dad was the parent who came back for me. My mother left the both of us. Left without a trace. He was the 'better' one. The best of the worst, right? And yet, here she is, in the flesh, her warmth seeping into my bones.

I find myself hesitating as I begin to hug her too, unsure of how to react.
I've never done the whole 'mum' thing before.

Glancing over her shoulder, I'm met with a tableau of stunned faces, each mirroring my own shock and disbelief. They too are grappling with the surrealness of this moment, their eyes wide with astonishment, their mouths agape in silent wonderment as they bear witness to the unfolding scene before them.

As she frantically pulls away, her trembling hands delicately stroke through my hair, her touch a tender caress laden with years of longing and regret. Tears stream down her cheeks, mingling with my own, as she steps back slightly to glare into my eyes, her expression a tumult of disbelief and overwhelming emotion.

"Oh, Marcus," she whispers, her voice trembling as she gently caresses my cheek. "I can't.. I can't believe this is really happening. You're really here."

I stand frozen in place, like a statue carved from stone, unable to tear my eyes away from her. As she continues to speak, I'm lost in a whirlwind of thoughts and emotions. I find myself lost in the labyrinth of my own thoughts, navigating through my memories. Memories long buried resurface, fragments of a past I've struggled to make sense of.

But amidst the overwhelming flood of her emotions, there's a sudden urgency in her face, a desperate plea masked by the veil of tears.

"Sweet," she continues, her voice trembling with apprehension, like a delicate leaf caught in the breeze of uncertainty. "Where's your brother? Is he okay?"

The question doesn't even compute in my brain. To say I'm overwhelmed would be an absolute understatement. The world around me blurs as my mind races to grasp the enormity of what has been asked of me. It's as though I've been thrust into a maze of memories I didn't know existed, each twist and turn revealing fragments of a life I never knew I lived.

Holy shit.

"I.. I have a brother?"

The story continues in..

'Brother's revenge.'

(THE FINALE)

Playlist

Chapter 1:

Swim – Chase Atlantic

Chapter 2:

Fluorescent Adolescent – Arctic Monkeys

Chapter 3:

Death with Dignity – Sufjan Stevens

Chapter 4:

Piano Fire – Sparklehorse

Chapter 5:

Santa Monica Dream – Angus & Julia Stone

Chapter 6:

Into It – Chase Atlantic

Chapter 7:

PAINT IT BLACK – Arankai

Chapter 8:

Mess Is Mine – Vance Joy

Chapter 9:

Something Good – alt-J

Chapter 10:

Daddy Issues – The Neighbourhood

ABOUT THE AUTHOR

Amber Fawn, born 2002, is a Cornwall-based indie author, specialising in Romance & Dark romance. Her passion for reading and writing began as early as 3 years old when she forced herself to learn how to read. Her preferred writing style is often on the darker side, experimenting with elements of gore and psychological trauma.

Website: amberfawnwrites.com
Instagram: @amberfawnauthor